Twisted Starr
The Final Chapter

Twisted Starr
The Final Chapter

BY

TRACY WILSON

Published by
Beautiful Publications LLC
Stratford, CT 06614

This book is a work of fiction. Names, characters, places, and incidents are either products of the author's imagination or are used fictitiously. Any resemblance to actual events or locales or persons, living or dead, is entirely coincidental.

PRINT ISBN: 978-1-7331792-7-0
EBOOK ISBN: 978-1-7334002-1-3

Printed in the United States of America

Dedication

I dedicate this series to Starr.

.

Chapter 1

"Hey Thompson – look at that pretty lil' thing right there..." Chandler said, pointing in my direction...

"She sure is pretty..." Officer Thompson agreed...

"To bad she 'about to be arrested..." Chandler sighed...

"For what? Being pretty isn't a crime..."

"Being pretty isn't a crime... but prostitution is..."

"Oh shit! Really?"

"Only one way to find out..." Chandler said as he got up, came outside and walked towards me. "Hello..." he said.

"Hi..." I responded coolly...

"You have nice eyes..."

"Thank you..."

"Can I buy you a cup of coffee?" he asked, hoping he could lure me into the diner...

"Sigh... sure... why not... looks like I missed my bus again..." I said as I turned towards him and looked at him.

"What time is the next bus?"

"Not for another hour."

"Come sit with me - I'll buy you dinner to go with your coffee..."

"That sounds nice – thank you..." I said as I walked towards him with a smile...

"Gotcha!" he thought to himself as I walked past him into the diner and sat at a table near the door....

"Shit – I'ma enjoy dinner, I'ma enjoy coffee, and I'ma be out!" I thought to myself as he came over to the table and sat down...

"What's your name?" he asked as he sat down..."

"Waitress – could you bring us some menus – and some coffee?" I asked, ignoring his question...

"Can I get your name... please?"

"Sure officer – as soon as I get yours..." I smiled.

"Here's your menus..." the waitress said as she came over to the table with the menus and a pot of coffee... "I'll be right back..." she said as she went to get two cups...

"Damn - was I that obvious?" he asked...

"Hell yea!" I laughed...

"Well..." he said as he leaned over and took my hand... "Thank you for allowing me to buy you dinner..." he said as he picked up my hand and kissed it...

"Ooohhh... an officer... and a gentleman... you get brownie points for that..." I blushed...

"Here's your coffee..." the waitress said as she placed the cups on the table and poured us coffee...

"May I?" he asked as he picked up the spoon and began pouring sugar into my coffee...

"Yes please..." I said as I made eye contact with him...

"How many would you like?" he asked, smiling mischievously...

"As many as you'd like to give me..." I answered, smiling mischievously. He over-poured three spoons of sugar into my coffee, opened three creamers, added them to my coffee, stirred it, then watched as I picked up the cup and started drinking it...

"Mmmm.... Perfect..." I breathed...

"Glad you like it..." he smiled as he over-poured three spoons of sugar into his coffee, opened thee creamers, added them to his coffee, stirred it, picked it up, and started drinking...

"Lose your partner..." I said. He spit his coffee back into his cup he laughed so hard...

"Yo Thompson – I'ma holla at you later..." he yelled across to Thompson...

"Aiight – Sarge – later..." Thompson said as he left the diner.

"Oooohhh... Sarge? As in Sergeant?" I asked...

"Yea..." he answered...

"Are you ready to order?" the waitress asked...

"Yes – I'll have a bacon cheeseburger deluxe – hold the coleslaw..." I said as I finished my coffee...

"I'll have the same..." he said as he finished his coffee...

"More coffee?" the waitress asked...

"No thank you..." I answered...

"None for me either..." he answered. The waitress left to place our orders and we made eye contact again...

"So... Sergeant... I'll tell you my name... if you'll tell me yours..." I said...

"Chandler..."

"Hmmm... Chandler... I like that..." I said as I smiled...

"So... who do I have the pleasure of dinning with this evening?" Chandler asked...

"Starr... my name is Starr..."

"Pleased to meet you Starr..." he said as he leaned forward and kissed me on the cheek...

"Nice meeting you too Chandler..." I blushed...

"You live around here?"

"I live about an hour away from here..."

"It takes you an hour to get home from here?"

"Yea..."

"So... are you just getting off work?"

"Kinda..."

"Kinda?"

"Yea..."

"So... where do you 'kinda' work?" he asked, emphasizing the word 'kinda' with his fingers...

"I don't really wanna talk about that..." I said putting my head down..."

"Sorry... we can talk about something else... if you want..." he said as he took my hand...

"I'm actually looking for a job..."

"Oh... Okay..."

"I'm on unemployment – but it's about to run out – I need to find something before it does..." I said...

"Well... you already know I'm a Sergeant..."

"Yes I know..." I said as I smiled...

"Have you ever thought about civil service?"

"Yea..."

"You ever take a civil service exam?"

"No..."

"You should – the pay is good – and so are the benefits..."

"I'm not sure I'm qualified..."

"As long as you don't have any felonies you're qualified..."

"Really?" I asked as the waitress came with our food and put it on the table...

"Oh yea – all you need is a high school or equivalency diploma for an entry level position – but you're getting unemployment so I know you have experience..." Chandler said as he picked up his burger and bit into it...

"Damn!" I laughed..."I thought I was hungry!"

"You ain't the only one – these burgers are slammin'!" he said as he took another bite...

"Oh damn – my bus just left – shit!"

"I'll make sure you get home..." Chandler said as he put his hand on mine...

"Okay... thank you..." I said as I picked up my burger and took a bite... "Oh my God!" I moaned...

"Told you!" Chandler laughed...

"So tell me about you..." I said as I continued eating...

"What would you like to know?"

"Well..." I said in between bites... "Are you single?"

"Are you interested?"

"Not really..." I answered as I started eating my fries. Chandler sat there quiet. "I was just playing Chandler – I'm sorry..." I said as I took his hand...

"Really?" Chandler asked...

"Really..." I answered...

"Yes... I'm single..."

"So am I... but I have a feeling that's about to change..." I smiled...

"Is that right?" Chandler asked as he finished his fries...

"Yea..." I smiled. Chandler smiled back at me making eye contact.

"Shall we get dessert?"

"Naaa... I always get disappointed when I order dessert from dinners..."

"Trust me..." Chandler said as he took my hand..."

"Okay..."

"Waitress?" Chandler called out...

"I'll be right there honey..." she answered as she finished taking an order at another table. We kept looking into each other's eyes without speaking until the waitress came over to the table...

"What can I getcha?" she asked...

"Two apple pie alamode..." Chandler answered...

"Ooohhh... that sounds good..." I breathed. Chandler and I took each other's hands and looked into each other's eyes as the waitress walked away to get our dessert. We didn't speak to each other but we rubbed each other's hands on the table. I knew this wasn't a good idea but when your body's been deprived, it seeks what it craves, his touch felt good, and I was starving...

"Here ya go..." the waitress said as she placed the apple pie and ice cream on the table...

"Thank you..." Chandler said as the waitress walked away...

"Mmmm..." I said as I tasted it... "You're right... this is good..."

"Told you..." he laughed as he started eating...

"You like that..."

"Like what?"

"Saying I told you so..." I laughed as I licked my spoon...

"Yea... I do..." he laughed as he took another spoonful of apple pie and ice-cream. I finished my plate, put my hands up under my chin, placed my elbows on the table, and watched Chandler finish his dessert. Chandler finished his dessert, took my hands from under my chin, and held them in his until the waitress brought the check to the table... "I guess I'll get you home now..." he said as he stood up from the table...

"I guess you will..." I said as I stood up. We both walked to the register, Chandler paid the check, and then we left the diner. "My car's right around the corner..." he said as he put his arm around me. I put my arm around him and we walked to his car. When we got to his car, he opened the door, waited for me to get in, and then closed the door. I reached over to the other side to unlock the door before he could open it...

"Thanks – but I have the key..." he laughed as he sat down and closed the door...

"I know..." I laughed. Chandler started the car, and then turned to look at me...

"Where to?"

"See that bus at the light?"

"Yea..."

"Follow that bus..."

"Follow the bus?"

"Yea – follow that bus..."

"It'll take me longer to get you home that way..." he laughed...

"I know..." I said as I took his hand. Chandler smiled, put the car in drive, and followed the bus. Every time the bus stopped, Chandler stopped, and each time he stopped, he looked over at me, smiling. This went on for about 45 minutes and then I spoke... "Stop here..."

"Okay..." Chandler said as he slowed down to a stop...

"Make a right..."

"Okay..."

"Make this next right..."

"Okay..."

"We're here..." I said as I let go of Chandler's hand and unbuckled the seat belt. I watched Chandler unbuckle his seat belt and I waited for him to open his door and get out the car. He closed the door, walked around to the front of the car to the passenger side and opened the door for me... "Thank you..." I said as I got out the car. When I stood up, Chandler closed the door and pulled me into a kiss before I could object, but I didn't object – I kissed him back as he pinned me against the car...

"Can I see you again?" he breathed...

"Yes... I'd like that..." I breathed as I moved out from underneath him...

"Can I come in?"

"Good night Chandler..." I laughed as I went upstairs. Chandler stood there watching me as I opened the door, went inside, and closed it. After I closed the door, I opened the window and stuck my head out... "You're still here!" I yelled...

"I never got your number!" he yelled...

"I know where you work! I'll call you!"

"Okay! Good night!" I watched Chandler get into his car and drive off, and then I closed my window. I started to go towards the kitchen but my phone rang, so I stopped to answer it...

"You have a collect call from an inmate at the Bridgeport Correctional Facility – will you accept the call?"

"Yes I will..." I said...

"Hey Starr..."

"Hey Mommy..."

"How'd everything go?"

"Oh Mommy... it was wonderful..." I sighed...

"Starr... please don't tell me... you fucked him – didn't you?"

"Not yet... but I'm going to..."

"Starr! What the hell's a matter with you?"

"Nothing!"

"Starr – I need you to stay focused!"

"Oh I'm focused alright..." I laughed...

"Dammit Starr! I didn't set this up for you to get some dick – I set this up so we could get revenge!"

"Well – I'ma get some dick whether you set it up or not..." I laughed...

"Starr... baby... please listen to your mother..."

"Mommy – you don't have to worry about me – I'm taking care of myself..."

"You're barely taking care of yourself – you don't have a job – please girl – you're all I have..." she said as she started crying...

"Please don't cry Mommy – I promise – I'm okay..." I said as tears formed in my eyes...

"You promise?"

"Yes Mommy – I promise..."

"Okay then – tell me about your date..."

"It went just like you said it would..."

"He saw you at the bus stop?"

"Yep."

"I knew it! Did he offer to buy you coffee?"

"Yep."

"That's his M.O. – he knows you're not a trick now..."

"Ma!"

"Starr – that's how they trap tricks – Officer Thompson sits in the diner, Sergeant Chandler offers to buy coffee, the trick offers pussy for money – next thing you know – bam!"

"Ma... are you saying he played me tonight?"

"No baby – I'm not saying that at all – if he wasn't interested in you he wouldn't have invited you into the diner..."

"Mommy?"

"Yea?"

"How'd you *know* he invited me into the diner?"

"You said your night was wonderful..."

"Yes... I did..."

"Mary – time's up!" I heard the Warden yell...

"Five more minutes... please..." my mother pleaded...

"Okay Mary – but don't make it obvious I gave you extra time – I'm gonna come back and act like you snuck extra time..."

"Okay – thanks..." my mom whispered...

"Tell me about your date Starr..."

"Mommy – we held hands, we ate, we laughed, and we kissed..."

"I love it when you're happy – but be careful baby..."

"I Will Mommy – he's gonna help me get a job..."

"No! You can't do that!"

"Why Mommy?"

"They fingerprint you and run a background check on you for civil service jobs..."

"Chandler says as long as I don't have any felonies I can get a job Mommy..."

"Starr – listen to me – they'll take your fingerprints – they'll do a background check – and they'll find out you're my daughter..."

"Oh shit – that's right – okay Mommy – I'll find another way..."

"Mary! Didn't I tell you time's up? Get off that phone – now!"

"I love you Starr!" my mom said as the call was disconnected...

"I love you too Mommy..." I whispered out loud as I hung up the phone...

Chapter 2

"How'd everything go the other night?" Thompson asked as Chandler walked in...

"Good morning Thompson..." Chandler said as he walked past Thompson back to his office...

"Wait a minute!" Thompson said as he stormed into Chandler's office...

"I'm not in the mood Thompson..."

"Did you hit it?"

"Not that it's any of your business – but no – I didn't..."

"What? Are you serious? Why not?"

"I like her..."

"My man Chan done fell for the mark... haaa... haaa!"

"Shut the fuck up Thompson!"

"Did you get her name?"

"Yea!"

"Did you get her phone number?"

"Not yet..."

"Not yet? Haaa.... Haaa.... Haaa... - guys – you gotta here this one..." Thompson laughed on his way out to the main area...

"What's up?" another officer asked...

"Chan fell for the mark..."

"Aww c'mon! Not you Chan! You been on the job for too many years to let this happen!" another officer laughed...

"So you didn't hit it?" another officer asked...

"When's the last time you hit something man – shut up!" Chandler snapped...

"He didn't even get her number!" Thompson laughed...

"Damn – no pussy –no number – just what did you get?" another officer asked...

"She'll call me..." Chandler answered...

"Bhaaaa.... Haaa.... Haaa...." The officers laughed...

"Your cards' been revoked!" one of the officers laughed...

"Hey Chan..." I said as I walked into the main area...

"Hey Starr!" Chandler beamed with pride as he stood up, come from behind the desk, and pulled me into a kiss...

"Is it okay if I call you Chan?"

"You can call me anything you want..." Chandler smiled...

"Are you free for lunch?"

"I sure am – I'll see y'all later – I'm out!" Chandler said as he wrapped his arm around me and we walked out the precinct...

"I'm surprised you came to the precinct..." Chandler said...

"I wanted to surprise you..."

"You did... you did... listen – I have something I need to ask you..."

"Oh boy – this sounds serious..."

"It is – come with me..." he said as he took my hand and led me to the parking lot. When we got to the squad car he opened the door for me to get in...

"I'ma get to ride in the squad car? Okay!" I beamed as I got in and Chandler closed the door. I watched Chandler walk around to the driver side and stand there. I reached over, unlocked the door, and Chandler opened it... "You lookin' good in that uniform officer..."

"Thank you..." he said as he got in the car and closed the door. I moved closer to Chandler and pulled him into a kiss, which surprised him... "You must be really happy to see me..."

"I am... especially in that uniform..."

"Maybe I should'a wore this the night I met you..."

"I'm glad you didn't..."

"Really?"

"Yea..."

"Why?"

"'Cause I got to fall for the man behind the uniform..." I said before I kissed him...

"Did you just say you fell? For me?"

"I did..."

"I love you too..." Chandler said as he touched my face...

"So... what did you want to ask me?"

"I want you to be my lady..."

"Okay... I'm your lady..."

"I have something for you..." he said as he reached in his pocket and pulled out a velvet box...

"What's this?" I asked as I smiled...

"Open the box..."

"Okay..." I gushed as I opened it... "Oh Chandler!"

"You like it?"

"I love it..." I whispered with tears in my eyes. Chandler watched as I went in my pocketbook, took out my keys, and added his key to my key ring.

"So... where can I take you for lunch?"

"Let's go to your place – I wanna use my new key!"

"Okay..." Chandler said as he put the car in drive and drove out the parking lot. When we got to his building I was in awe...

"Wow – right downtown – this is nice..."

"Wait 'till you see inside..."

"I have..."

"You have?"

"Yea – they have pictures of the lofts online..." I said as he parked the car...

"C'mon – let's go – I can't wait for you to see it..." Chandler said as he got out the car and closed the door. Instinctively I got out the car and closed the door... "Why'd you do that?"

"I thought you were in a hurry..."

"I am – but – never mind – let's go!" he said as he took me by the hand and pulled me towards the building...

"Hey Chan..." the doorman said as Chandler pulled me inside...

"Hey..." Chandler said as he pulled me to the elevator. When the doors opened, Chandler took me by the hand and pulled me inside the elevator. I watched him push the button for the 15th floor and smiled...

"I bet the views are beautiful..." I said...

"You're about to find out..." Chandler said as we got to the 15th floor and the elevator doors opened. Chandler took my hand and led me out the elevator to his loft...

"Now... where's my key – here it is!" I beamed as I put the key in the lock and opened the door... "Oh my God! It's beautiful!"

"Thank you..." Chandler said as he closed the door. The panoramic views were just as beautiful as I imagined. Chandler had a 3 bedroom, 2.5 bath end unit with an oversized living room, floor-to-ceiling windows, a wrap-a-round balcony, laundry room, and a semi-private elevator.... "Make yourself at home – I'll be in the kitchen..." Chandler said as I walked around the loft... "Starr?"

"Yes Chan?"

"Come join me on the balcony..."

"Okay..." When I got out onto the balcony Chandler had set a table with wine and a platter with cheese, crackers, grapes, strawberries, and cantaloupe. I sat down at the table and Chandler stood there with his arms folded... "I'm sorry..." I said as I stood up and backed away from the table. This time, I waited for Chandler to pull the chair out for me before I sat down...

"I'on know who you were with before – but you're gonna have to get used to me being a gentleman and treating you like my lady – understand?"

"I'm sorry – it's just that I've been alone for so long, it's just habit – and Mommy always says... never mind..."

"Naaa... finish... what does your mother say?"

"She says I gotta learn to take care of myself..."

"She right..." Chandler said as he took some more food and another sip of wine... "You do have to learn to take care of your self – and you have – and now you need to learn another lesson..." he said as he came over to me and pulled me up from the chair...

"What lesson is that?" I breathed as he pulled me close to him and started kissing me on my neck...

"You... need... to... learn... how... to... let... me... love... you..." he said in between kisses on my neck and shoulders before he pulled my face to his and kissed me fully...

"Mmmm.... I'm really enjoying this lesson..."

"Oh shit – that's my phone – hold that thought..." he said as he ran to get his phone... "Yea... uh huh... I'm on my way..." I waited for him to come back on the deck to tell me what I already knew... "I have an emergency – they

18

need me to come back — stay here — I'll see you later tonight..." he said and then he kissed me, grabbed his keys, and flew out the door...

"Hmmm... let me see what's in that closet..." I said as I went into the master bedroom... "Ooohhh..." I said as I took a uniform shirt off the hanger and put it on the bed. I stood at the end of the bed, stripped naked and looked at myself in the mirror...

"Whatcha lookin' at Sarge?" Thompson asked as he walked up behind Chandler...

"Nothing — do you need something?" Chandler snapped as he turned his phone down...

"Oh... I get it... you finally got that phone number... and she sent you a text..."

"Yea..." Chandler smiled...

"Sorry about earlier — we still good?"

"Sorry my ass!"

"It's just that..."

"It's just that y'all are choking on the shit you was talkin' 'cause you thought I lost it — talkin' 'bout my cards' been revoked — I started the mutha fuckin' club — I own the mutha fuckin' club!"

"I'll see you later..." Thompson laughed as he walked away and Chandler went back to watching...

"I like the way this looks on me..." I said as I buttoned the shirt...

"So do I..." Chandler said as he continued watching...

I climbed up on the edge of the bed, flopped back on it with my arms and legs spread wide, closed my eyes, and enjoyed the comfort of the bed and pillows...

"Mmmm... I can't wait to get in between those legs... and kiss you from the bottom of that tattoo all the way up to the center of your pleasure..." Chandler said as he watched until I fell asleep...

"Ohhh..." I said as I yawned and stretched... "Damn that was a good nap – I wonder what time Chandler's getting here?" I said as I got up and went into the kitchen.... "Hmmm... chicken cutlet – okay – what else?" I said as I looked in the cabinets... "Egg noodles... okay – oh wait – pasta salad – yes!" I said as I took the pasta salad down out the cabinet and put it down on the counter... "Okay – vegetables – what's going on in this fridge... collard greens – it'll do – I sure hope he has seasoning..." I said as I started looking in the cabinets... "Adobo, Grill Mates Montreal Chicken Seasoning – jackpot! Now if he has olive oil I'm good... and... he has it! Now I'ma see if I can get this done before he gets home...

"Hey Thompson – come take a look at this..." Chandler said...

"Watcha lookin' at this time?" Thompson asked as he walked over to Chandler and peeked over his shoulder... "Oh shit – you're spying on her?"

"No I'm not spying on her – just watch..."

"Ooohhh... she making you dinner... nice..." Thompson said as he fist-bumped Chandler...

"And I didn't even have to ask her..."

"Damn – How'd you know she was the one?"

"First, I offered to buy her coffee, which she accepted. Second, I offered to buy her dinner with her coffee and she accepted. Third, she let me take her home... and now... she's making me dinner... and I'm about to get up outta here..." Chandler said as he stood up to leave...

"Hi Mommy!" I said cheerfully as I answered my cell...

"Hey Starr – what has you so happy?"

"Not what Mommy – who..."

"Oh? Tell me..."

"Mommy..." I sighed...

"Awww... you're in love... who is he?"

"I'm sorry Mommy..."

"Sorry for what?"

"It's Chandler..."

"Starr! Noooo!"

"Please don't be mad Mommy..."

"Starr... baby girl... I love you with all my heart... but you have a tendency to see the world through those beautiful blue eyes of yours – and it's going to get your heart broken..."

"Mommy... he loves me..."

"Oh my poor baby – please listen to me Starr..."

"Mommy... I love you with all my heart – you know that right?"

"Yes baby – but..."

"Mommy?"

"Yes Starr..."

"If I'm wrong about him – I'll let you say I told you so..."

"That's what you said about what's-his-name – I can't even remember – but that mutha fucka hurt you – and you cried – and I told you so – and you didn't like it..."

"You're right Mommy..."

"Chandler is a very persuasive man – and I need you to stay focused..."

"Mommy?"

"Sigh... yes Starr..."

"Just because I'm in love doesn't mean I won't stay focused – I'm just focused on Chandler right now..."

"That's exactly what I'm afraid of..."

"Mommy – you don't understand..."

"Starr?"

"Yes Mommy?"

"I was your age once too ya know..."

"Oh so you understand perfectly then..." I laughed as I finished setting the table on the deck and went inside to check on the food...

"Yes I do – you're lonely, you have needs, and right now... Chandler is giving you what you need..."

"Yes Mommy... he is..."

"Are you sure he's the one? That's how you felt about what's-his-name – what was his name?"

"Warren..."

"Right!"

"Mommy... Warren was immature... Chandler is..."

"Let me stop you right there – you're immature too..."

"Mommy!"

"I just mean you're still young – and Chandler is a bit older than you..."

"We were talking about you earlier today..."

"Who? You and Chandler?"

"Yes Mommy... he gets upset when I don't let him open doors for me or pull out chairs for me – so I told him you said I have to learn how to take care of myself..."

"Damn right! What'd he say?"

"He said he don't know who I was with before but I better start letting him be a gentleman and treat me like his lady... and Mommy – guess what else he said?"

"What Starr?"

"He said I need to learn how to let him love me..."

"Well I'll be... maybe I was wrong about him..."

"Told ya!" I laughed...

"Starr – I just want you to be happy – it makes me happy to hear you so happy – but I still want you to be careful..."

'I'll try Mommy... but when I'm near him I can't control myself..."

"Oh God – Starr – don't mess around and get pregnant – that's the last thing you need right now – you still takin' the pill?"

"Oh my God – Mommy – don't you think I'm a little old for this talk?" I laughed...

"As long as you need to hear it – you're never too old..." my mom laughed...

"Mommy?"

"Yes Starr?"

"I'm not taking any pills...

"Starr!"

"Mommy – I'm not having sex... yet..."

"What about Warren?"

"What about him?"

"Are you still a virgin?"

"Yes Mommy – I'm still a virgin..." I sighed...

"So you and Chandler haven't..."

"No Mommy – we haven't..." I interrupted... "But we're going to..."

"I guess you've waited long enough huh?" my mom laughed...

"Ya think?" I laughed...

"Mary – time's up!" I heard the Warden say...

"I gotta go – I love you Starr..."

"I love you too Mommy..."

"Damn it smells good in here!" Chandler said as he came in...

"Hey Chan..." I said when I saw him...

"C'mere..." he said. I went over to him and he pulled me into a kiss...

"You must be happy to see me..." I breathed...

"Very..." he breathed before pulling me into another kiss...

"Ummm... you hungry?" I asked nervously...

"Kinda sorta..." Chandler laughed as he took off his holster, took off his jacket, and laid them both down on the table in the foyer...

"Can we eat outside?"

"Sure... if you want..."

"Okay – I'll make the plates and bring them outside..."

"Okay..." Chandler said as he went out onto the deck and sat at the table...

"Hmmm... he's actually letting me make the plates..." I mumbled as I made the plates and brought them outside. I set the plates down on the table and folded my arms...

"Something wrong?"

"Nope..." I answered as I smiled...

"Why aren't you sitting down then?"

"I'on know who you were with before – but I'ma let you be a gentleman and treat me like your lady!" I laughed...

"Oh... my bad..." he laughed as he got up, pulled out the chair for me, I sat down, and then he sat down...

"I had a nice nap today..." I said as we started eating..."

"I know..."

"You know? How?"

"I saw you..."

"You saw me? Oh my God – you were spying on me?"

"Starr - wait – let me explain..."

"I can't believe you were spying on me! Why'd you bother giving me a key if you don't trust me?" I asked as I stood up and started to go inside but Chandler got up and grabbed me... "Let go of me!"

"No!" he said as he grabbed me into a hug...

"Let me go!"

"I'ma let you go – but you're gonna sit down and let me explain – understand?"

"What if I don't want to?"

"I'm not letting you go unless you agree to listen to me..."

"Okay..." I said as I sat down...

"I wasn't spying on you..."

"But you were watching me..."

"Yes... I was..."

"Why?"

"Because you're beautiful..."

"So... did you see everything?"

"Are you asking me if I saw you naked?"

"Yea..."

"Yes…"

"How often do you do that?"

"Starr – you know I'm a Sergeant right?"

"Yea…"

"So… in my career I've put a lot of people behind bars… and sometimes they get out… so I keep my place under surveillance for my protection…"

"Okay…" I sighed…

"The cameras are set to record automatically whenever there's movement and I'm away – so when there's movement it records…" I sat there and finished eating without saying anything… "Are you okay?"

"Yea…"

"No you're not – what's wrong?"

"I wasn't ready for you to see me naked…" Chandler got up from the table, came over to me, pulled me up into his arms, and held me…

"I'm sorry…"

"I know…"

"I can let you see me naked if that'll make you feel better…"

"I'm not sure…"

"You're not sure? I don't understand…"

"I haven't been with anyone…" I said as I turned my head away from him…

"You're a virgin?"

"Yea…"

"Starr… look at me…" I couldn't look at him…

"Starr..." he whispered as he picked up my chin... "Look at me..." When he saw the tears in my eyes he kissed me...

"I don't want to disappoint you..." I whispered...

"I'm the one that needs to be worried..." he said before kissing me again...

"You? Why?"

"I need to make sure your first time is special..." he said as he picked me up in his arms... "And I don't want to disappoint you..." he said as he carried me into the bedroom. When we got to the bedroom, Chandler laid me on the bed. I'll be right back..." he said as he left the bedroom. I wasn't sure where he went until I heard music playing and I realized he had music coming through the speakers. He came back into the bedroom, dimmed the lights, and stood at the end of the bed, making sure to take his time taking off his clothes so I could see him completely nude. I started blushing and he knew I liked what I saw so he climbed up on the bed and lay down next to me. Freddie Jackson's 'You Are My Lady' started playing and Chandler started unbuttoning his shirt I was wearing as he started signing to me... "There's something that I want to say... but words sometimes get in the way..." He opened the shirt, wrapped his arm around me, and pulled me close to him as he sang... "I just want to show you my feelings for you..." I wrapped my arm around him and pulled myself even closer so I could feel his erection against me as he continued singing... "There's nothing that I'd rather do... then spend every moment with you... I guess you should know I love you so..." I started to cry and he wiped my tears as he continued singing... "You are my lady... you're everything I need and more... you are my lady..." he sang as I continued crying... "You're all I'm living for..." he sang as he wiped my tears. Chandler started kissing me and we continued kissing as Freddie sang...

"There's no way that I can resist... your precious kiss... girl you've got me so hypnotized...

"Just say that you'll stay with me..." Chandler sang...

"I'll stay..." I said as Chandler wiped my tears...

"Because our love was meant to be... I promise to love you more each day..." Chandler sang, and then he let Freddie finish the song as he started making love to me...

"Hey Starr..." he said as I yawned and stretched...

"Hey Chan... I said as I yawned and stretched...

"How are you feeling?"

"Wonderful..." I sighed...

"Good..." Chandler said and then he kissed me...

"Can we do it again?"

"We can do it as much as you like..." Chandler said as he climbed up on top of me, spread my legs, and eased himself inside me... "Are you okay?"

"Yes... I'm okay..." I said as I closed my eyes...

"Open your eyes..."

"Okay..." Chandler spread my legs wider, wrapped his arms around me, and instead of being on the bottom, I was now on top of him. I pushed myself up and looked down at Chandler and smiled as I realized he was deep inside me. Chandler could tell I was excited but he also knew it was awkward for me so he held on to my hips and started thrusting up while moving my hips back and forth until I got the rhythm. I braced myself on his shoulders with the palms of my hands and Chandler held my hips as I moved back and forth...

"Oh Chan... I'm cumming..." I moaned...

"Go right ahead..." he breathed...

"Ohhhh..... Ohhhh..... Ohhh..... Oooohhhhh!!!" Chandler slowed down but didn't stop – he continued thrusting inside me until my orgasm subsided...

"Was it good?"

"Yea... it was good..." I breathed...

"Good..." he said as he grabbed me and flipped me on my back...

"Chan..." I moaned as he started thrusting harder..."

"Am I hurting you?"

"No..." I breathed...

"Okay..." he said as he continued thrusting harder... "Shit... I'm cumminnn.... Umph... Umph... Umph... Ummmppphhh!" Chandler collapsed on top of me and started kissing me.

We continued kissing as he lay there between my legs… "I love you Starr…"

"I love you too Chan…"

"You wanna get some dessert?"

"I'd love to…"

"Okay — let me get you a towel so you can clean up and then we'll go in the kitchen. I waited for Candler to come back with the towel, wiped between my legs, and I wasn't prepared for what happened next…

"Oh my God… I'm bleeding!"

"That's normal…"

"It is?"

"Yea — you were a virgin…"

"I know — but I didn't think it would be that much… sorry I messed up your towel…"

"I have more towels — c'mon — let's go get some dessert…

"Oh shit — I gotta go!"

"Where do you think you're going?" Chandler said as he pushed me back down…

"I have to go… if I don't show up tomorrow…"

'Tomorrow?"

"Yea…"

"Is this about that work thing that you didn't really wanna talk about?" Chandler asked as he propped himself up on his elbow and looked at me…

"Yea…"

"Can't you go to work from here?"

"I could — I just need to figure out how to get the bus from here…"

"I'll make sure you get to work..." Chandler interrupted...

"I'm not working..."

"I know..."

"You do?" I asked as I turned to face him...

"Anybody that has a work thing that they don't wanna talk about is doing one of two things – they slingin' or they're going to DSS – and I know you're not slingin' – so you wanna tell me what's going on?"

"I have to recertify for Section 8..."

"Okay – what time do you need to be there?"

"My appointment is tomorrow morning at 8 a.m."

"I'll make sure you get there on time..." he said as he started kissing me on my neck... "Now... about dessert..." he said as he pulled me to him and kissed me... "What would you like?"

"You..." I breathed as I kissed him back... "I'd like some more... of you..."

"Coming right up..." Chandler said as he climbed up on top of me, spread my legs, eased himself inside me, and began making love to me again.

Chapter 3

"Good morning..." Chandler whispered in my ear as he kissed me awake...

"Mmmm.... Good morning... what time is it?"

"6 a.m...."

"Oh my God... I'm sleepy..." I yawned...

"It's time to get up..." Chandler said as he got up, climbed on top of me, spread my legs, and started kissing me...

"Are you going to wake me up like this every morning?" I breathed...

"I could... if you want me to..." Chandler started licking and sucking my left breast and then my right...

"Ooohhh.... Chandler..." I moaned. Chandler kissed me down my body, past my stomach... and then he stopped. He got up on his knees and looked me in my eyes. I was excited and wet, anticipating what he was going to do next... and then he spoke...

"So... tell me..." he said as he picked up my leg... "about this tattoo..." and then he started kissing and licking my ankle...

"I... I..." I breathed... "I got it when I was... 16..."

"Did… it… hurt?" he asked between kisses and licks as he moved up my leg…"

"Mmmm… no… it's Henna…" I moaned as he continued kissing and licking up my leg…"

"What's… Henna?" he asked as he sucked on my thigh…

"Ooohhh… it's… no… needles…" I moaned as he put my leg down, lay down between my legs, and spread my lips…

"Chandler… ooohhh…" I moaned as he began flicking his tongue up and down on my clit. I was scared of what I was feeling but I didn't want him to stop either…

"Mmmm….." Chandler moaned as he stuck his tongue inside me and licked and sucked…"

"Oh Chandler… Chandler… Chandler…" I moaned as I tossed my head back and forth and grabbed his head. Chandler began alternating between licking and sucking inside, licking and sucking my clit, and licking and sucking my lips… and it was making me come… "Chandler… I'm coming… I'm coming…" Chandler stuck two fingers inside me and sucked my clit hard as my legs started shaking, I clenched his head with my legs… and I screamed… "Chaaaannnnnn!" as I came really hard… and peed on his face. Chandler stopped, lifted up his head, and looked at me. I was embarrassed when I saw Chandler's face dripping from me peeing on him but Chandler wiped his face with his hand and went back to licking and sucking on my clit and my lips softly… "Chandler…" I whispered. Chandler didn't pay me any mind — he just continued licking and sucking... "Chandler... I... I.... it's... sensitive..." I breathed. Chandler continued licking and sucking for a bit longer and then he came up between my legs, eased his dick inside me, and began kissing me as he started thrusting, and I could taste myself... "Mmmm..... Mmmmm..... Mmmmm..." I moaned as he began thrusting harder and faster...

"Mmmph! Mmmph! Mmmph!"

"Mmmm..... Mmmmm..... Mmmmm..."

"Mmmph! Mmmph! Mmmph!"

"Mmmm..... Mmmmm..... Mmmmm..."

"Mmmph! Mmmph! Mmmph! Mmmph! Mmmph!" Chandler collapsed on top of me and continued kissing me for a few moments... and then I spoke...

"Yes..." I breathed...

"Huh?" Chandler asked before he kissed me again...

"Yes... I'd like... you... to... wake... me... up... like... this... every... morning..."

"Okay..."

"I need to... get... in... the... shower..."

"I'll... come... with... you..."

"Okay..." I breathed. We both got up; Chandler took me by the hand, and led me to the shower. I waited for Chandler to step into the shower and turn on the water before I joined him. Chandler pulled me into a kiss and held me against him as the water beat down on us... "I gotta hurry up..." I said as I pulled away from him... but Chandler ignored me... and pulled me right back into his arms and held me...

"Just let me hold you..."

"Okay... I said as I closed my eyes and let the water hit my face and body... and then I felt the washcloth between my legs... "That tickles..." I laughed. Chandler washed up and down all over and then reached for the shampoo, squirted some in his hands, and washed my hair... "Mmmm..." I moaned as he massaged my scalp before rinsing my hair out. He reached for the conditioner, squirted some in his hands, and began massaging my scalp again... "Oh my God... that feels so good..." I moaned as he continued massaging my scalp and then, before rinsing my hair again he pushed me back, spread my legs, and began making love to me standing up... "Oohhh! Oooohhh! Ooohhh!" I moaned as I wrapped my arms around his neck and held on...

"Mmmph! Mmmph! Mmmph!"

"Oohhh! Oooohhh! Ooohhh!"

"Mmmph! Mmmph! Mmmph!"

"Chandler... I'm cumming... I'm cumming..."

"Mmmph! Mmmph! Mmmph! Mmmph! Mmmph!" I relaxed my legs but I didn't let go of him as he kissed me...

"Your turn..." I breathed...

"Okay..." Chandler said and reached for the soap. We kept our eyes on each other as I washed him from his head down to his waist. I looked down and saw he still had an erection so I squatted down to wash his dick. Chandler watched intently as I deliberately took my time washing his dick, stroking it as I did so, and then I washed the rest of him and stood back up... "Do you like what you see?"

"Yes... very much..."

"Do you like how it makes you feel?"

"Yes... very much..."

"Do you want some more?" Chandler asked as he turned off the water and guided me out the shower and back into the bedroom...

"Yes... but I need to get dressed..."

"Yea... it's about 7:30 – we better hurry..." he said as we started getting dressed. I looked at the wet spot on the bed and I immediately felt ashamed... "What's wrong?"

"I'm sorry..." I said as I turned away from him...

"Sorry about what? That?" he asked as he pointed to the bed...

"Yea..."

"Don't worry 'bout that..." he said as he pulled me close to him... "I don't mind golden showers...

"Really? I'm so embarrassed..."

"Why?"

"I've never done that before..."

"You've never done that?"

"No... you were the first..."

"Okay – now I understand..."

"You do?"

"Once you get used to it – you won't pee – but don't worry about it – I don't mind golden showers..." he said and then he kissed me...

"I love you..."

"I love you too – let's get downstairs and get you to your appointment..." he said as he grabbed my hand, grabbed his keys, grabbed my bag, and we hurried out the door. When we got downstairs the squad car was parked in front so we didn't have to go to the parking lot. Chandler hurried around to the passenger side and opened the door for me and then hurried back around to the driver's side. After he started the car, it didn't take us more than 10 minutes and we were there... "Can I get a kiss before you go?"

"Is it okay if we don't?"

"Why?"

"I don't want these people in my business – sometimes the caseworkers hang around outside and report everything they see – somebody'll tell Ms. Cox they saw me getting out of your car – watch..." I said as I started to open the door...

"Don't you dare!"

"Okay..." I sighed. Chandler got out the car, came around to the passenger side, opened the door for me, and I got out... "Thank you Officer!" I said deliberately.

"You're welcome – have a good day!" Chandler said before he got back in his car and drove off. While I was standing in line waiting for DSS to open, I took out my cell phone and sent him a kissing emoji. Chandler took out his phone, looked at it, smiled, and sent me one back.

"Mommy!" I exclaimed when my phone rang...

"Oh my God – you did it!"

"Mooommmyyyy!"

"That good huh?" my mother laughed...

"Mooommmyyyy!"

"Can you talk?"

"Hold on Mommy..."

"Starr Osgood – window 2..."

"Here!" I yelled as I ran to the window...

"Ms. Cox is running late – you'll be seen but it'll be closer to 9 a.m. – is that okay or do you want to re-schedule?"

"Oh no – I'll wait..."

"You'll wait?" Oh wow – I'm surprised you don't have an attitude..." the receptionist laughed...

"I have an attitude – a good one!"

"Wow – I wish all our client's had your attitude – it would make our job so much easier..." she said as I found a corner to sit in so I could talk to my mother...

"Mooommmyyyy!"

"Dammit Starr – what happened?"

"Mommy..." I said as I started crying...

"Starr? Why are you crying?"

"He sang to me Mommy..." I said as I started crying harder..."

"Aww..."

"He made me feel so good Mommy..."

"Oh Starr... this... this is what I wanted for you..."

"I'm so glad I waited Mommy..."

"Told ya!"

"Yes Mommy – yes you did... I was embarrassed... I didn't know what to expect... but he... he..."

"I know baby... I know..."

"He loves me Mommy... he really loves me..."

"I'm so happy for you Starr..."

"I love him Mommy..."

"I know you do..."

"Mommy?"

"Yes?"

"I did something..."

"What did you do baby?"

"It's embarrassing..."

"You can tell me Starr..."

"I... I... peed..."

"You what?"

"I peed..."

"When?"

"When he... I can't say it..."

"Starr?"

"Yes Mommy?"

"It's okay..."

"That's what Chandler said..."

"It was your first time... you didn't know what to expect..."

"Mommy?"

"Yes?"

"It wasn't my first time..."

"I don't understand..."

"Mommy..."

"Yes?"

"We did it the first time... I went to sleep... I woke up... we did it again... and again... I went back to sleep... we did it again this morning... and we did it again in the shower..." I didn't hear anything. I thought we got disconnected... "Mommy? Are you still there?"

"Yes baby... I'm still here..." she whispered as she started to cry...

"Mommy! Don't cry!"

"It's okay baby... I'm crying because I'm happy..."

"I'm happy too Mommy..."

"Starr?"

"Yes Mommy?"

"Are you going to tell him the truth?"

"Yes Mommy – I'm gonna tell him after I see Ms. Cox..."

"Good... I never thought it would turn out this way... but I'm glad it did..."

"Me too Mommy..."

"Starr?"

"Yes Mommy?"

"Did he use condoms?"

"No..."

"Starr! What the hell's a matter with you?"

"Nothing Mommy..."

"What if you're pregnant?"

"If I'm pregnant – then I'll be having a baby with the man I love..."

"Starr – Noooo!"

"Mommy!"

"Starr – you need to stay focused – you're struggling right now – you don't have a job – oh my God – I knew it – I should've never set this up..."

"I'm glad you did..."

"What?"

"Mommy – you set me up with a good man – a Sergeant – he's fine – he's got good dick – he can have any woman he wants – and he chose me – he loves me – and I love him – what did you think was gonna happen?"

"To be honest – I didn't think he was gonna fall for you..."

"Mommy!"

"Let me explain..."

"Okay..."

"I knew he was a good man – I knew he would be nice to you – I knew he would help you – I just didn't think he would fall for you – but now you're telling me you didn't use condoms and he went down on you – he did go down on you right?"

"Yes Mommy..."

"Now I know he really loves you – and you might be pregnant – and it worries me..."

"Why Mommy?"

"Because... when I got pregnant with you... things changed..."

"Oooohhh.... Mommy?"

"Yes Starr?"

"You're not gonna have to worry about me for too long..."

"Oh my God..."

"What's wrong Mommy?"

"You sound just like your father..."

"Wayne?"

"No... Bazil..."

"Starr Osgood – window 2..."

"Mommy – I gotta go – I love you..."

"I love you too Starr..."

"Here..." I said when I reached the window..."

"Thanks for waiting – go over to the interview room right there – I'm coming now..."

"Okay Ms. Cox..." I said as I walked over to the interview room. "Come with me..." she said as she opened the door and held it open for me to go inside. I went in and sat down. She came in behind me, closed the door, and sat behind the desk...

"I need to ask you something... and I need you to tell me the truth..."

"Okay..."

"Did you get out of a squad car this morning?"

"Yea..." I laughed...

"What's so funny?"

"Nothing – it's just... never mind..."

"Are you in trouble?"

"No Ms. Cox..."

"Call me Crystal – Ms. Cox is out there..."

"Okay... Ms. Crystal..."

"Why were you in the squad car?"

"I missed the bus and the officer gave me a ride so I would be here on time..."

"Hmmm... that's it?"

"Yes Ms. Crystal..."

"You know if you get in trouble you lose your Section 8 right?"

"Yes Ms. Crystal... I know..."

"Okay... so have there been any changes since you last recertified?"

"I'm still trying to find a job – but it's hard..." I sighed...

"I know – but don't give up..."

"My unemployment is about to run out... what if I don't find a job?"

"As long as you continue to report and keep your work search appointments – you'll be fine..."

"Oh thank God!" I breathed... "Will I be able to get food stamps?"

"Yes – if you don't have a job you can get food stamps and cash – it's not much – but you can get it – I looked over your file – you've been doing everything we told you – I'm proud of you – I know how hard it's been – especially with everything you're dealing with..."

"Thank you Ms. Crystal..." I smiled.

"How's your mother doing?"

"She's up for parole – I think she's getting out this time – then she can come stay with me..."

"Sigh – I'm sorry to tell you this.... but your mother can't stay with you..."

"Why?" I asked as I started crying..."

"Your mother has a felony – you live in public housing – if you let your mother stay with you I have to report it – and you'll forfeit your Section 8..."

"That's not right – it was her Section 8 – I only got it because she added me to her lease..."

"I'm glad she did that for you – you'll be okay..."

"Where's my mom supposed to go?" I cried...

"Your mom's going to have to go to a shelter... and wait for placement..." she said as she handed me tissues...

"I can't let my mother go into a shelter – this isn't right – I'll just have to forfeit my Section 8..." Crystal got up from the table, pulled the chair next to me, sat down, pulled me into a hug, and held me as I cried on her shoulder...

"Starr?"

"Yes Ms. Crystal?"

"Listen to me..." she said as she picked up my face by my chin and looked me in my eyes... "You'll do no such thing..."

"But..."

"Starr..." she interrupted...

"Yes Ms. Crystal?"

"If your mother were here right now – what would she tell you?"

"She would tell me to stay focused and don't worry about her..."

"And that's exactly what you're going to do... understand?"

"Yes Ms. Crystal..." I sniffed...

"Your mom's been in prison – trust me – she can take care of herself – the shelter is a country club compared to jail..."

"It's not fair — she shouldn't have to live like that…"

"She won't be there for long Starr…"

"Can she come visit me?"

"Starr — it's not jail!" she laughed…

"So can she spend the night?"

"Yes Starr — she can spend the night — but not every night…

"Can she spend the weekend?"

"Starr — you need to focus on yourself — you start worrying about your mother you'll stop making progress — you've come too far — I know this is hard to hear — but your mother would want you to listen to me…"

"I know…"

"Once you find a job, maybe you can afford a place of your own without Section 8 — then your mother can come stay with you — but apartments are expensive — you might still qualify for Section 8 even if you're working — and you need to hang on to your Section 8 as long as you can — okay?"

"Yes Ms. Crystal…" I said with my head down…"

"Uh uh — look at me…" she said as he picked my head up by my chin…"

"Yes Ms. Crystal?"

"You're gonna be okay — hang in there…" she said as she gave me a hug… "Come back and see me in three months — and continue to keep your other appointments…"

"Okay Ms. Crystal… bye…" I said as I got up and left…

"Ms. Cox speaking – how may I help you?"

"Ms. Cox – this is Sergeant Corbett from Bridgeport – how are you?"

"I'm fine – what can I do for you?"

"I'm calling regarding one of your clients – Starr... I don't know her last name..."

"Oh - that's easy – I only have one client named Starr – is she in trouble?"

"Oh no – her name came across my desk – I'm trying to help her get a job – I'm just calling to verify what she told me...

"Sergeant Corbett – did you give Starr a ride to this office earlier today?"

"Yes I did – why?"

"I thought she was in trouble – good to know she was telling me the truth..."

"She's a good girl..."

"Yes she is – I'm so proud of her – she's been able to keep her head on straight and stay focused all this time – even with her mother in prison..."

"Her mother's in jail?"

"Yea – it's a long story..."

"Tell me... I got time..."

"Her mother used to work for Osgood Publishing – and she got arrested for embezzlement – good thing she added Starr to her Section 8 or Starr would've been out on the street..."

"Yes... that is a good thing..."

"Yea – she's been through a lot – her step-father raised her until she was 18 – he bounced after he found out he wasn't her real father..."

"Oh damn..."

"Yea – once he found out Bazil Osgood was her father he just bounced..."

"Bazil Osgood?"

"Yep..."

"Send me her file..."

"Okay Sergeant – I'll get it right over to you..."

"This can't be happening right now..."Chandler said out loud...

"What's wrong Sarge?" Thompson said as he walked into Chandler's office...

"You wouldn't believe me if I told you..."

"Try me..." Thompson said as he pulled up a chair and sat down...

"That pretty lil' thing I've been seeing?"

"Yea? What about her?"

"She's Bazil Osgood's daughter..."

Chapter 4

"You're right... I don't believe it..." Thompson said...

"I need you to do something for me... and keep it between us..."

"Sure Sarge..."

"Get me the phone calls between Mary Smith and Starr..."

"Mary Smith? The one that embezzled money from Bazil Osgood?"

"Yea..."

"Oh my God... That's her mother... Isn't it?"

"Yea..."

"I'm on it Sarge..." Thompson said as he took off and Chandler began reading the file...

"Hmmm... so far everything checks out..." he said as he read through the file. When he got to the birth certificate he read it meticulously:

Mother: Mary Smith
Father: Bazil Osgood
Child: Starr Smith Osgood
Date of Birth: February 3rd, 1997

Chandler continued reading and stopped to go over the unemployment logs, job searches, etc. "Everything checks out – I see why Ms. Cox is so proud of her..." Chandler said as he smiled. "Hmmm.... let me check a lil' further..." Chandler said as he logged on to the computer and looked up looked up Bazil Osgood. "Hmmm... let's print a copy of Bazil's medical records..." he said as he printed them out... "Okay – now to compare it to Starr's drug and alcohol assessment... damn..." Chandler sighed as he looked back and forth between the medical records, compared the blood work and DNA, and realized Bazil was definitely Starr's father...

"I'm back Sarge..." Thompson said as he came inside and gave Chandler the recordings...

"Everything checks out... so far..." Chandler said as he smiled.

"Thank God – I couldn't take it if she broke your heart – this is the happiest I've seen you in a long, long time..." Thompson laughed...

"Don't thank me for shit – I never sanctioned what you did to those girls!" God said...

"I'll let you in on a secret..." Chandler said as he pulled a blue velvet box out of his pocket...

"Sarge! You're gonna propose?"

"I was..."

"You changed your mind?"

"No..."

"I don't understand..."

"I'm an old-fashioned man..."

"You mean you gonna get on bended knee, etc."

"No..." Chandler laughed... "I need to ask her father for his blessing before I ask her to marry me..."

"Bhaaaa! Haaa! Haaa! Sarge... stop it..."

"I'm serious..."

"Oh shit!"

"Yes..."

"So... you're going to see Bazil... you're going to tell him you're fuckin' his daughter, and then you're going to ask for his blessing? Are you crazy?"

"I love her. I need to get her father's blessing..."

"Oh you'll get his blessing alright - Bazil's gonna know your head clean off!" Thompson laughed...

"It's possible..."

"You gonna arrest him?"

"No..."

"Why not?"

"I'm a man – he's a man – and this is his daughter we're talkin' about – it has nothing to do with his past..."

"Damn Sarge – I gotta give it to you – in fact – I've never respected you more than I have in this moment – I'm proud to be in your command..." Thompson said as he stood up and saluted Chandler...

"At ease – let me get to these recordings – I'll see you later – and Thompson?"

"Yea Sarge?"

"This stays between us…"

"Got it!" Thompson said as he left Chandler's office…

"Now… let's get started…" Chandler said as he started the first recording. Chandler could feel his heart sinking into his chest as he continued listening…

"You have a collect call from an inmate at the Bridgeport Correctional Facility – will you accept the call?"

"Yes I will…"

"Hey Starr…"

"Hey Mommy…"

"How'd everything go?"

"Oh Mommy… it was wonderful…" I sighed…

"Starr… please don't tell me… you fucked him – didn't you?"

"Not yet… but I'm going to…"

"Starr! What the hell's a matter with you?"

"Nothing!"

"Starr – I need you to stay focused!"

"Oh I'm focused alright…"

"Dammit Starr! I didn't set this up for you to get some dick – I set this up so we could get revenge!"

"Starr… noooo…." Chandler whispered…

"Well – I'ma get some dick whether you set it up or not…"

"Starr... baby... please listen to your mother..."

"Mommy – you don't have to worry about me – I'm taking care of myself..."

"You're barely taking care of yourself – you don't have a job – please girl – you're all I have..."

"Please don't cry Mommy – I promise – I'm okay..."

"You promise?"

"Yes Mommy – I promise..."

"Okay then – tell me about your date..."

"It went just like you said it would..."

"He saw you at the bus stop?"

"Yep."

"I knew it! Did he offer to buy you coffee?"

"Yep."

"That's his M.O. – he knows you're not a trick now..."

"Ma!"

"Starr – that's how they trap tricks – Officer Thompson sits in the diner, Sergeant Chandler offers to buy coffee, the trick offers pussy for money – next thing you know – bam!"

"Ma... are you saying he played me tonight?"

"No baby – I'm not saying that at all – if he wasn't interested in you he wouldn't have invited you into the diner..."

"Mommy?"

"Yea?"

"How'd you now he invited me into the diner?"

"You said your night was wonderful..."

"Yes... I did..."

"Mary – time's up!"

"Five more minutes... please..." my mother pleaded...

"Okay Mary – but don't make it obvious I gave you extra time – I'm gonna come back and act like you snuck extra time..."

"Okay – thanks..."

"Tell me about your date Starr..."

"Mommy – we held hands, we ate, we laughed, and we kissed..."

"I love it when you're happy – but be careful baby..."

"I Will Mommy – he's gonna help me get a job..."

"No! You can't do that!"

"Why Mommy?"

"They fingerprint you and run a background check on you for civil service jobs..."

"Chandler says as long as I don't have any felonies I can get a job Mommy..."

"Starr – listen to me – they'll take your fingerprints – they'll do a background check – and they'll find out you're my daughter..."

"Oh shit – that's right – okay Mommy – I'll find another way..."

'Mary! Didn't I tell you time's up? Get off that phone – now!"

"I love you Starr!" my mom said as the call was disconnected...

"I love you too Mommy..."

"Starr... I love you so much... why would you do this to me?" Chandler whispered as he started to cry.

Chapter 5

"Hey Chan..." I said as I ran up to him, hugged him, and tried to kiss him... but he pushed me away...

"Sit down..." Chandler said...

"Baby... what's wrong?" I asked with tears in my eyes...

"Was any of it real? Or was it all a lie?" Chandler asked as he started crying...

"Chandler... please...   What's wrong?" I asked as I started crying. Chandler started the recording:

"You have a collect call from an inmate at the Bridgeport Correctional Facility – will you accept the call?"

"Yes I will..."

"Hey Starr..."

"Hey Mommy..."

"How'd everything go?"

"Oh Mommy... it was wonderful..."

"Starr... please don't tell me... you fucked him – didn't you?"

"Not yet... but I'm going to..."

"Starr! What the hell's a matter with you?"

"Nothing!"

"Starr – I need you to stay focused!"

"Oh I'm focused alright..."

"Dammit Starr! I didn't set this up for you to get some dick – I set this up so we could get revenge!"

"Well – I'ma get some dick whether you set it up or not..."

"Starr... baby... please listen to your mother..."

"Mommy – you don't have to worry about me – I'm taking care of myself..."

"You're barely taking care of yourself – you don't have a job – please girl – you're all I have..."

"Please don't cry Mommy – I promise – I'm okay..."

"You promise?"

"Yes Mommy – I promise..."

"Okay then – tell me about your date..."

"It went just like you said it would..."

"He saw you at the bus stop?"

"Yep."

"I knew it! Did he offer to buy you coffee?"

"Yep."

"That's his M.O. – he knows you're not a trick now..."

"Ma!"

"Starr – that's how they trap tricks – Officer Thompson sits in the diner, Sergeant Chandler offers to buy coffee, the trick offers pussy for money – next thing you know – bam!"

"Ma... are you saying he played me tonight?"

"No baby – I'm not saying that at all – if he wasn't interested in you he wouldn't have invited you into the diner..."

"Mommy?"

"Yea?"

"How'd you now he invited me into the diner?"

"You said your night was wonderful..."

"Yes... I did..."

"Mary – time's up!"

"Five more minutes... please..."

"Okay Mary – but don't make it obvious I gave you extra time – I'm gonna come back and act like you snuck extra time..."

"Okay – thanks..."

"Tell me about your date Starr..."

"Mommy – we held hands, we ate, we laughed, and we kissed..."

"I love it when you're happy – but be careful baby..."

"I Will Mommy – he's gonna help me get a job..."

"No! You can't do that!"

"Why Mommy?"

"They fingerprint you and run a background check on you for civil service jobs..."

"Chandler says as long as I don't have any felonies I can get a job Mommy..."

"Starr – listen to me – they'll take your fingerprints – they'll do a background check – and they'll find out you're my daughter..."

"Oh shit – that's right – okay Mommy – I'll find another way..."

'Mary! Didn't I tell you time's up? Get off that phone – now!"

"I love you Starr!" my mom said as the call was disconnected...

"I love you too Mommy..."

"Chandler... please... I can explain..."

"I love you so much Starr..."

"I love you too... please... let me explain..."

"I can't trust you... you need to go..."

"Chandler please... don't do this..."

"You did this Starr..."

"Okay... I'll leave... if that's what you want..."

"Make sure you leave my shirt..."

"Fine – but ya know what?"

"What?"

"You're not exactly innocent either..."

"Whatchu mean?"

"You thought I was a whore..."

"I didn't want you to be a whore... but you wanted me to help you get revenge... right?"

"Chandler... please... if you just let me explain..." I said as I tried to touch him...

"Uh uh – get your things – leave my shirt – and go – I need time to think!"

"Okay..." I whispered as I got my back, dropped his shirt on the couch, and left. Chandler didn't know I had another shirt in my bag.

"How could I be so wrong about her?" Chandler said as he sat in his chair and cried.

When I got home I broke down crying as soon as I closed the door... "Oh God! Please! I love him so much!" I cried as I slumped down to the floor... and then my phone rang...

"You have a collect call from an inmate at the Bridgeport Correctional Facility – do you accept the charges?"

"Yes... I accept..."

"Hey baby girl..."

"Mommmyyy!" I cried...

"Oh Starr... what happened?"

"He... he..."

"You told him?"

"He told me to leave Mommy! He doesn't love me anymore! Oh God – Mommy it hurts!"

"Wait a minute – he doesn't understand?"

"Mommy – he has a copy of our phone call – the one where you set us up – now he thinks I don't love him..."

"Oh my God... baby... I'm so sorry..."

"I need him Mommy!" I cried...

"I know baby..."

"I'm gonna beg him to take me back..."

"No Starr..."

"Yes Mommy! I never should'a listened to you!"

"Starr... I never meant for you to get hurt..." my mother said as she started to cry...

"Please don't cry Mommy – I'm sorry..."

"No baby – I'm sorry..."

"I need his help Mommy – Ms. Crystal gave me some bad news today..."

"Oh no... what'd she say?"

"She said you can't come stay with me because I live in public housing and you have a felony – if you come stay she'll report it and I'll lose my Section 8..." I cried...

"Baby... it's okay... I already knew that..."

"Mommy? Why didn't you tell me?"

"Because baby – I can take care of myself – I need you to stay focused – let me take care of me..."

"Mommy – I don't want you to live in a shelter – I want you to come home!" I cried...

"Starr – listen to me..."

"No..."

"Starr?"

"Yes Mommy?"

"I will be okay – at least in the shelter you can come see me – I can feel your arms around me and you can feel mine around you..."

"I need that Mommy... you're all I have now..."

"You have Chandler too..."

"Mommy... he was so hurt... he was crying Mommy..."

"Damn – he really loves you..."

"No Mommy... he hates me..."

"No baby... he still loves you... that's why he cried..."

"Mommy that doesn't make any sense!" I laughed...

"Did Warren cry when y'all broke up?"

"No..."

"See? Chandler cried – he still loves you..."

"I hope so Mommy..."

"I know so..."

"Mommy?"

"Yes Starr?"

"I'm going to see my father..."

"Starr! No!"

"Mommy I need his help!"

"I know you do – but I don't want you to go see him..."

"Mommy – my unemployment is about to run out – I haven't found a job yet – Ms. Crystal said I could get food stamps and cash but it won't be much – I don't know what else to do Mommy..."

"Okay..."

"So you won't be mad if I go see my father?"

"No baby – but can you do me a favor?"

"Yes Mommy..."

"Wait a couple of days..."

"Why Mommy?"

"Because Chandler's coming to see you..."

"I hope so Mommy..."

"Mary – time's up!"

"I gotta go – bye Starr – I love you!"

"I love you to Mommy!" I said as I hung up and started praying:

"God – please help me – I'm trying really hard – but I'm struggling – I need a job – I need my mother – I need my father... and... I need Chandler..."

"He'll be here soon..." God answered. I took off my clothes, pulled Chandler's shirt out my bag, put it on, climbed in bed, and cried myself to sleep.

Chapter 6

"Hey Sarge..." Thompson said as he walked into Chandler's office...

"Hey..." Chandler said...

"Oh shit – what happened? And don't say nothing 'cause it's all over your face...

"It's over..." Chandler whispered as tears fell down his face...

"No Sarge it isn't..."

"She broke my heart..."

"Naaa... there must be something going on..."

"Here!" Chandler said as he threw the recordings at him...

"What's this?"

"I only listened to the first one – and I heard everything I needed to hear...

"What did you hear?"

"They set me up..."

"They? Who's they?"

"Starr... and her mother..."

"What? Why?"

"I don't know!"

"Sarge?"

"What?"

"Did you listen to everything?"

"I heard what I needed to hear..."

"Sarge..."

"Dammit Thompson – leave me the hell alone!" Thompson came in, closed the door... and locked it... "I said..."

"I don't give a damn what you said Sarge..."

"That's it – I'm writing..."

"Oh shut up!" Thompson yelled...

"Do you know who the hell you're talking to Thompson?"

"I did – but now I'm not so sure..."

"Move! Now!" Chandler said as he got up...

"I'm not moving unless you agree to listen to everything..."

"Why do you give a damn?"

"Because she makes you happy..."

"I can't – give me the damn recordings..."

"Here!" Thompson laughed as he threw them back at Chandler...

"Aiight – I'ma listen to everything – and you're gonna leave me the hell alone – okay?"

"Okay!" Sarge said as he smiled got up, and closed the door.

"Le'me get this over with..." Chandler said as he started listening to the second recording:

"Hi Mommy!"

"Hey Starr – what has you so happy?"

"Not what Mommy – who..."

"Oh? Tell me..."

"Mommy..."

"Awww... you're in love... who is he?"

"I'm sorry Mommy..."

"Sorry for what?"

"It's Chandler..."

"She does love me..." Chandler said with tears in his eyes...

"Starr! Noooo!"

"Please don't be mad Mommy..."

"Starr... baby girl... I love you with all my heart... but you have a tendency to see the world through those beautiful blue eyes of yours – and it's going to get your heart broken..."

"Mommy... he loves me..."

"Oh my poor baby – please listen to me Starr..."

"Mommy... I love you with all my heart – you know that right?"

"Yes baby – but..."

"Mommy?"

"Yes Starr..."

"If I'm wrong about him – I'll let you say I told you so..."

"That's what you said about what's-his-name – I can't even remember – but that mutha fucka hurt you – and you cried – and I told you so – and you didn't like it..."

"You're right Mommy..."

"Chandler is a very persuasive man – and I need you to stay focused..."

"Mommy?"

"Sigh... yes Starr..."

"Just because I'm in love doesn't mean I won't stay focused – I'm just focused on Chandler right now..."

"That's exactly what I'm afraid of..."

"Mommy – you don't understand..."

"Starr?"

"Yes Mommy?"

"I was your age once too ya know..."

"Oh so you understand perfectly then..."

"Yes I do – you're lonely, you have needs, and right now... Chandler is giving you what you need..."

"Yes Mommy... he is..."

"Are you sure he's the one? That's how you felt about what's-his-name – what was his name?"

"Warren..."

"Right!"

"Mommy... Warren was immature... Chandler is..."

"Let me stop you right there – you're immature too..."

"Mommy!"

"I just mean you're still young – and Chandler is a bit older than you..."

"We were talking about you earlier today..."

"Who? You and Chandler?"

"Yes Mommy... he gets upset when I don't let him open doors for me or pull out chairs for me – so I told him you said I have to learn how to take care of myself..."

"Damn right! What'd he say?"

"He said he don't know who I was with before but I better start letting him be a gentleman and treat me like his lady... and Mommy – guess what else he said?"

"What Starr?"

"He said I need to learn how to let him love me..."

"Well I'll be... maybe I was wrong about him..."

"Told ya!"

"Starr – I just want you to be happy – it makes me happy to hear you so happy – but I still want you to be careful..."

"I'll try Mommy... but when I'm near him I can't control myself..."

"She really loves me..." Chandler whispered as he continued listening...

"Oh God – Starr – don't mess around and get pregnant – that's the last thing you need right now – you still takin' the pill?"

"Oh my God – Mommy – don't you think I'm a little old for this talk?"

"I can't believe her mother thinks Starr is still a lil' girl..." Chandler laughed as he continued listening...

"As long as you need to hear it – you're never too old..."

"Mommy?"

"Yes Starr?"

"I'm not taking any pills...

"Starr!"

"Mommy – I'm not having sex... yet..."

"What about Warren?"

"What about him?"

"Are you still a virgin?"

"Yes Mommy – I'm still a virgin..."

"So you and Chandler haven't..."

"No Mommy – we haven't..."but we're going to..."

"I guess you've waited long enough huh?"

"Ya think?"

"Mary – time's up!" I heard the Warden say...

"I gotta go – I love you Starr..."

"I love you too Mommy..."

"She chose me... she wants me... Oh Starr... " Chandler whispered as he began listening to the third recording...

"Mommy!"

"Oh my God – you did it!"

"Mooommmyyyy!"

"That good huh?"

"Mooommmyyyy!"

"Can you talk?"

"Hold on Mommy..."

"Starr Osgood – window 2..."

"Here!"

"Ms. Cox is running late – you'll be seen but it'll be closer to 9 a.m. – is that okay or do you want to re-schedule?"

"Oh no – I'll wait…"

"You'll wait?" Oh wow – I'm surprised you don't have an attitude…" the receptionist laughed…

"I have an attitude – a good one!"

"Wow – I wish all our client's had your attitude – it would make our job so much easier…"

"Mooommmyyyy!"

"Dammit Starr – what happened?"

"Mommy…" I said as I started crying…

"Starr? Why are you crying?"

"He sang to me Mommy…" I said as I started crying harder…"

"Aww…" Chandler said, crying as he continued to listen…

"Aww…"

"He made me feel so good Mommy…"

"Oh Starr… this… this is what I wanted for you…"

"I'm so glad I waited Mommy…"

"Told ya!"

"Yes Mommy – yes you did… I was embarrassed… I didn't know what to expect… but he… he…"

"I know baby… I know…"

"He loves me Mommy… he really loves me…"

"Yes Starr… I really love you…" Chandler whispered, crying as he continued to listen…

"I'm so happy for you Starr..."

"I love him Mommy..."

"I know you do..."

"Mommy?"

"Yes?"

"I did something..."

"What did you do baby?"

"It's embarrassing..."

"You can tell me Starr..."

"I... I... peed..."

"You what?"

"I peed..."

"When?"

"When he... I can't say it..."

"Oh my God... she told her mother..." Chandler whispered as he continued listening...

"Starr?"

"Yes Mommy?"

"It's okay..."

"That's what Chandler said..."

"It was your first time... you didn't know what to expect..."

"Mommy?"

"Yes?"

"It wasn't my first time..."

"I don't understand..."

"Mommy..."

"Yes?"

"We did it the first time... I went to sleep... I woke up... we did it again... and again... I went back to sleep... we did it again this morning... and we did it again in the shower..."

"Oh my God... I can't believe she's telling her mother... Starr..." Chandler whispered as he continued listening...

"Mommy? Are you still there?"
"Yes baby... I'm still here..."
"Mommy! Don't cry!"
"It's okay baby... I'm crying because I'm happy..."
"I'm happy too Mommy..."
"Starr?"
"Yes Mommy?"
"Are you going to tell him the truth?"
"Yes Mommy – I'm gonna tell him after I see Ms. Cox..."

"She was going to tell me the truth... and I didn't give her a chance... Starr... I'm so sorry..." Chandler whispered, crying as he continued to listen...

"Good... I never thought it would turn out this way... but I'm glad it did..."
"Me too Mommy..."
"Starr?"
"Yes Mommy?"
"Did he use condoms?"
"No..."
"Starr! What the hell's a matter with you?"

"Nothing Mommy..."

"What if you're pregnant?"

"If I'm pregnant – then I'll be having a baby with the man I love..."

"Yes... you'll be having a baby with the man you love... I like that..." Chandler said as he smiled...

"Starr – Noooo!"

"Mommy!"

"Starr – you need to stay focused – you're struggling right now – you don't have a job – oh my God – I knew it – I should've never set this up..."

"I'm glad you did..."

"What?"

"Mommy – you set me up with a good man – a Sergeant – he's fine – he's got good dick – he can have any woman he wants – and he chose me – he loves me – and I love him – what did you think was gonna happen?"

"Tell her Starr!" Chandler exclaimed...

"To be honest – I didn't think he was gonna fall for you..."

"Mommy!"

"Let me explain..."

"Okay..."

"I knew he was a good man – I knew he would be nice to you – I knew he would help you

— I just didn't think he would fall for you — but now you're telling me you didn't use condoms and he went down on you — he did go down on you right?"

"Damn! Oh well Mommy... now you know!" Chandler laughed as he continued listening...
"Yes Mommy..."
"Now I know he really loves you — and you might be pregnant — and it worries me..."
"Why Mommy?"
"Because... when I got pregnant with you... things changed..."
"Oooohhh.... Mommy?"
"Yes Starr?"
"You're not gonna have to worry about me for too long..."
"Oh my God..."
"What's wrong Mommy?"
"You sound just like your father..."
"Wayne?"
"No... Bazil..."
"Starr Osgood — window 2..."
"Mommy — I gotta go — I love you..."
"I love you too Starr..."

"I was right about her... thank God..."
"You're welcome..." God said...
"Sarge? Can I come in?"
"Yea Thompson — come on in..."
"You okay?"
"Yea..." Chandler smiled...

"Aww shit – I knew it!"

"Yes you did…"

"Hate to – actually no – I love to say I told you so!" he laughed…

"Yes – you told me so – and I'm glad you did – thank you!"

"You're welcome Sarge – now… I have just one question…"

"What's that?"

"What the hell are you still doing here?"

"You're right!" Chandler said as he jumped up from his desk, grabbed his keys, and ran out his office…

Chapter 7

"Beautiee... I gotta go..."

"What's wrong?" Beautiee asked...

"I just got a text from Chandler – he said he needs me to meet him at the Galaxy Diner on Main Street – he says it's urgent!"

"I don't trust this Bazil... what if it's a set up?"

"Chandler wouldn't do that..."

"What makes you so sure?"

"If I were being arrested he would just tell me to meet him at the station – he doesn't play games..."

"It's late..."

"I know – I'll be back as soon as I can..." Beautiee walked towards Bazil, pulled him close to her, and started kissing him on his neck... "Mmmm... this feels nice... but I gotta go..."

"Can I get some dick before you go... please... My Thirst Quencher?" Bazil held Beautiee and walked her backwards towards the bed. Bazil undressed Beautiee, undressed himself, and then pushed Beautiee down on the bed... "Turn over and get on your knees..." Bazil commanded...

"Yes My Thirst Quencher..." Beautiee breathed as she obeyed his command. Her legs started trembling as Bazil got on the bed on his knees, pulled her by her hips, and started fucking her from behind... "Oh Bazil..." she moaned...

"Is this what you want?"

"Yessss Bazil... Yeesss..." she moaned. Beautiee was turned on by the sound of her ass smacking against Bazil and he knew it...

"Damn... your pussy's so fuckin' wet..."

"Your dick feels so good Bazil... fuck!"

"Tell me again..." Bazil breathed in her ear as he held her tighter and fucked her harder...

"Your dick feels so fuckin' good... Fuck me!" Bazil got up on his knees, pulled Beautiee's hair, and fucked her deeper... "Oh God... Oh God... Bazil... I'm cumming! I'm cumming!"

"Uggh! Uggh! Uggh! Uggh! Uggh!" Bazil and Beautiee both collapsed on the bed and Bazil kissed Beautiee on her neck and nibbled on her ear...

"Damn Bazil..." Beautiee breathed... "That was so good... can I have some more when you get back?"

"I'm up for it if you are..." Bazil breathed...

"I don't know what's gotten into me lately... I'm horny all the time..."

"I don't know what's gotten into you lately either... but I like it..." he breathed in her ear...

"Can't we just lay here and act like you didn't get Chandler's text?"

"I want to... more than you know... but I gotta go..."

"I know… I just wish you didn't have to…" Bazil turned Beautiee on her back, lay between her legs, and kissed her deeply… "Mmmm… you keep that up you ain't goin' anywhere…"

"I'll be back as soon as I can… and I'll give you more…"

"Hurry back Bazil… please…"

"I will…" Bazil said as he got up, grabbed his clothes, and headed downstairs. Beautiee was asleep before he headed out the door…

"Why does Chandler want to meet me here?" Bazil asked out loud as he parked the car and got out. "Oh well… I guess I'm about to find out…" he said as he walked into the restaurant…

"Bazil – over here…" Chandler called out. Bazil saw Chandler and went to sit at the table.

"What's this about Chandler?"

"Waitress – coffee please?" The waitress came over and poured two cups of coffee…

"Chandler… what's this about?" Bazil asked again…

"Sugar?" Chandler asked…

"Yes… thank you…"

"Cream?"

"Yes… thank you… I'm waiting Chandler…" Chandler didn't say anything. He started drinking his coffee and looked Bazil in the eyes. Bazil knew it was serious but he didn't say anything – he just picked up his coffee and drank it…

"Thanks for having coffee with me…" Chandler said…

"You're welcome…"

"This is hard…"

"I know…"

"How?"

"Because I know you Chandler…"

"Yes you do Bazil…"

"So… do I need to order something or are you gonna tell me why you invited me here at this hour?"

"Bazil…"

"Yes Chandler?"

"I need to talk to you about Starr…"

"Why would you need to talk to me about Starr?"

"She's your daughter…"

"You called me to the diner to tell me I have a daughter?"

"Yes… and no…"

"Chandler…"

"Bazil… just wait a minute…"

"Okay…"

"Starr is your daughter…"

"How do you know Starr's my daughter?"

"We have your DNA and blood tests from when you went to prison… we have Starr's DNA and blood tests from when she went for a drug & alcohol assessment – it's a match…"

"Why did my daughter need a drug & alcohol assessment?"

"Bazil…"

"Oh God… Chandler…"

"She's been struggling…"

"Chandler... please don't tell me..." Bazil whispered as he started to cry...

"Bazil... listen... please..."

"Okay..."

"Wayne left Starr to fend for herself when she was 18..."

"Oh my God... why?"

"He left her because he found out you were her father..."

"Why didn't she reach out to me? Why didn't Mary reach out to me?"

"You know why Mary didn't reach out to you..."

"How has Starr been surviving?"

"Before Mary went to jail, she added Starr to her Section 8 certificate so Starr would have a place to stay. Starr had a job but she lost her job - her unemployment is about ready to run out – and she hasn't found another job yet."

"Where is she living?"

"She lives in public housing down town in Bridgeport." Bazil sat there for a few minutes digesting everything Chandler said... and then it hit him like a ton of bricks...

"You're fuckin' my daughter... aren't you?"

"Yes Bazil... yes I am..." Bam! Bazil punched Chandler in the jaw and he hit the floor...

"Oh my God – are you alright – do you want me to call the police?" the manager asked as he came running over to help Chandler up off the floor...

"I am the police!" Chandler laughed as he sat back at the table with Bazil. Bazil was seething. His chest was heaving up and down and his nostrils were flaring... "Man to man – I'ma let you have that – as her father – I get it – you have this image in your mind of me turning your daughter out – but it wasn't like that – she gave herself to me – she chose to be with me – and I'm in love with her..."

"You're in love... with my daughter?"

"Yes Bazil..."

"How did you meet?"

"Mary set us up..."

"Mary?"

"I found out Starr was struggling so I asked the Section 8 worker to send me her file – I wanted to help her get a job – that's when I found out she was your daughter..."

"So you didn't know she was my daughter in the beginning?"

"No..."

"How did Mary set you up?"

"You know how Thompson and I get whores?"

"Oh God – Chandler... no..."

"Mary sent your daughter to the diner to get close to me... so she could get revenge on you..."

"How do you know all this?"

"After I looked at Starr's file, I pulled the calls between Mary and Starr. I listed to the recording and I thought Starr was using me... and it broke my heart..."

"You really love her…"

"Yes Bazil… I told her to leave – Thompson was the one that convinced me to listen to all the conversations…"

"Why does he even care?"

"Because he knows Starr makes me happy…"

"How do I know you won't get bored with my daughter and move on to the next? How do I know you won't break her heart?"

"Because I wouldn't be sitting here telling you all this…"

"I can't believe that Mary would put her daughter up to this – but I'm not surprised…"

"She's up for parole…"

"Fuck her!"

"Starr wants her mother to come home – but Mary has a felony – she's going to have to go to a shelter – Starr is very upset – she worries about her mother constantly…"

"Fuck her!" Bazil said again as he pounded his fist on the table…

"Okay Bazil – okay – I just wanted to let you know everything…"

"I need to see her…"

"I was hoping you'd say that…"

"Why?"

"Go to this address – I'll have them let you in…" Chandler said as he got up from the table…

"Where are you going?"

"I'll meet you there!" Chandler yelled as he paid the check and ran out…

"Yes Mr.   Chandler?" the   doorman answered...

"Bazil Osgood is on his way to my place – please let him in when he arrives...

"Sure thing Mr. Chandler."

Chapter 8

"Who is it?" I asked as I went to the door...

"Chandler..." I snatched the door open as fast as I could... Chandler came inside, picked me up, and I wrapped my legs around him as we started kissing fiercely. Chandler pushed the door closed, carried me to the bed, and laid me down with my legs still wrapped around him. We continued kissing as Chandler managed to get his holster off, get his pants off, and get his dick inside me...

"Hmmm..... Hmmm..... Hmmm... Hmmm..."

"Mmph! Mmph! Mmph! Mmph!"

"Hmmm..... Hmmm..... Hmmm... Hmmm..."

"Mmph! Mmph! Mmph! Mmph!" Chandler felt so good I started to cry and Chandler kissed my face, my tears, and my mouth...

"Chandler... Chandler... Chandler..."

"Starr... shit... damn this pussy good..." he said as he held me tighter and fucked me harder...

"I'm cumming..."

"I'm cumming with you..."

"Ohhh.... Ohhh... Ohhh... Ohhh..."

"Uggh!   Uggh!   Uggh!   Uggh! Uuuuggghhh!"   I started crying again and Chandler wiped my tears as he kissed me...

"I'm sorry Chandler..."

"I'm sorry Starr... I should've let you explain..."

"I was trying to tell you earlier tonight..."

"I know..."

"I haven't found a job yet..."

"I know..."

"My mother's getting paroled and I have Section 8 and..." Chandler deliberately put his tongue in my mouth and kissed me fully so I couldn't talk... "Mmmm..." I moaned as we continued kissing...

"Now..." he said as he kissed me again... "I need you to listen to me..."

"Okay... I breathed...

"I know everything..."

"You do?"

"Yes..."

"How?"

"I spoke to Ms. Cox. I asked her to send me your file. I was trying to help you...

"Oh Chandler..." I cried... "I love you so much..."

"I love you too..." he said as he kissed me again... "Now listen..."

"Okay..."

"I know Bazil Osgood is your father... and I had a talk with him..."

"Chandler..." I cried...

"I need to ask you something... and I need you to tell me the truth..."

"Okay..."

"Your mother said she set this up to get revenge..."

"My mother wants to get revenge on my father..."

"What do you have to do with that?"

"I just want a relationship with my father — but my mother wants revenge..."

"Starr?"

"Yes Chandler?"

"Do you really love me?"

"Yes Chandler..."

"Tell me..."

"I love you Chandler..."

"Tell me again..." Chandler said as he started kissing my neck...

"I... love... ooohhh...."

"You... love... oooohhh?" Chandler laughed...

"I love you... Chandler... I love you..."

"I know..."

"You do?"

"Yes Starr... I know you love me..." Chandler said as he continued kissing my neck... "Because you gave yourself to me..."

"Do you love me Chandler?"

"Yes Starr... I love you..." he said as he kissed my shoulders... "I love you..." he said as he opened his shirt I was wearing and kissed my left nipple... "I love you..." he said as he kissed my right nipple... "I love you..." he said as he kissed my stomach... "I... love... you..." he said as he spread my legs and began licking and sucking...

"Oooohhh... Chandler..." I moaned as I arched my back... Chandler lifted me up by my ass as he swirled his tongue around my clit... "Chandler... Chandler... Chandler..." I moaned as he continued swirling his tongue around my clit... and then he stuck his tongue inside me... "Ooohhh!" I moaned as Chandler held me up off the bed, spread my lips apart with his nose, and shook his head back and forth while licking and sucking harder... "Ccchhhhaaannddddlllleeerrrr!" I screamed as I arched my back and my legs trembled... Chandler continued licking and sucking softly as my orgasm subsided... sliding his tongue inside, and then licking outside... "Chandler..." I moaned... Chandler paid me no mind as I continued to experience mini orgasms with each flick of his tongue... "Ooohhh... Ooohhh... Ooohhhh..." Chandler grabbed my legs and pulled me down as he continued licking... sucking... and slurping... "Mmmm..." he moaned as he swirled his tongue around my clit... "Chandler... wait..." I panted... Chandler stopped, looked up at me, and I could see my juices on his mouth and chin...

"You want me to stop?"

"Yes... it's sensitive..."

"Okay..." he said as he came up my body while staying between my legs... and kissed me fully. This was my second time I was tasting myself on his lips... and I liked it... "Mmmm... you like when I kiss you after..." he said and then he put his tongue in my mouth... and I sucked it... "Mmmm... something new... okay... gimmie that..." I stuck my tongue in his mouth and he sucked it... and it turned me on...

"Get on your back..." I said...

"Okay..." Chandler said as he flipped me over and I was on top of him. I pushed myself up off him and Chandler looked at me as I got up on my knees. I started to move down between Chandler's legs and as I took Chandler's dick in my hands he stopped me... "Are you sure? You don't have to..." he said as he played with my hair. I didn't answer him... I took his dick in my mouth... slowly... "Starr..." Chandler moaned. I'd never done this before and it was awkward but when I heard Chandler moan it turned me on and I wanted to please him so I took him in my mouth a little further... "Starr..." he moaned again and I felt more confident as I started sucking his dick... "Starr... yes... suck it..." I loved hearing him talk to me that way and I loved knowing that I was making him feel good so I got on my knees, braced my upper body on his thighs, and continued sucking his dick, taking him all the way in my mouth and pulling him back out... "Starr... Ooohhh.... Shit..." I used my right hand to hold the bottom of his dick and I sucked the top of his dick a little harder while using my tongue... "Got damn... Starr... you goin make me cum... shit..." I was so turned on by what he said and I wanted to make him feel good

88

so I kept going... "Starr... wait... I'm... I'm..." Chandler realized I wasn't going to stop and he grabbed my head with his hands and started fucking my mouth... "Fuck! I'm cumming!" He came in my mouth and I swallowed it. I couldn't taste it but it felt warm against my throat. "Starr..." Chandler whispered as he played in my hair. I continued sucking his dick softly as his erection went down. I knew he felt good and I was happy. "Starr..." he whispered again...

"Yes..." I answered as I looked up at him...

"C'mere..." I moved up his body, he pulled me into a kiss, and kissed me hard...

"Was it good?"

"Hell yea..." he breathed...

"I wanted to make you feel good..."

"You did... you did..."

"I wasn't sure if I was doing it right... that was my first time..."

"That was just right..." Chandler said as he pulled me into another kiss..."C'mon – get dressed – I have a surprise for you..." Chandler said as he jumped up off the bed...

"Okay!" I squealed as I jumped up outta bed, we both got dressed, and headed to Chandler's place.

Chapter 9

"Starr – let me open the door..." Chandler said as he got in front of me...

"Okay..." Chandler opened the door and Bazil was sitting on the sofa. "C'mon in Starr..." Chandler said as he held the door open for me...

"Oh my God..." I whispered when I saw my father...

"Starr..." my father whispered as he stood up... came over to me... pulled me into a hug... and cried – and I cried right along with him...

"Daddy..."

"I know..."

"It's... been... so... hard..." I cried between sobs...

"I'm... sorry..." Bazil cried between sobs. Chandler watched us as we held each other and cried. "I'm gonna make it up to you Starr... I promise..."

"I wanted to reach out to you..."

"Why didn't you?"

"I wanted to try and do it on my own... but I need help Daddy..."

"I know... I wish I knew... I would've helped you..."

90

"You're not mad at me?"

"Starr... I love you..."

"But you thought Wayne was my father..."

"Yes I did..."

"And you still loved me? Why?"

"I knew there was a chance I was your father... I never stopped thinking about you..."

"Why didn't you ever tell me?"

"Sit down Starr..." my father said as Chandler brought tissues... "Your mother begged me not to tell you I could be your father..."

"Why? Why would she do that?"

"When your mother got pregnant I was married to her best friend."

"Mommy knew you were married to her best friend... and Mommy still got pregnant by you?"

"Yes Starr..."

"Mommy didn't tell me that..."

"Starr... listen to me..."

"Okay..."

"I was just as much to blame in that situation – it takes two..."

"Okay..."

"Wayne always wanted children and your mother didn't want to hurt Janet so I promised your mother I wouldn't tell Wayne he wasn't your father...

"That wasn't the only reason... was it?"

"Starr..."

"Daddy – tell me the truth... please..."

"Sigh... I didn't want to hurt Janet..."

"You mean you didn't want to lose Janet... right?"

"Yes..."

"So... you slept with my mother, got her pregnant, sent her to jail for stealing from you, then you killed her best friend – no wonder my mother hates you..."

"Starr... please... it wasn't like that..."

"Daddy..."

"Starr... please listen..."

"Okay..."

"I loved my wife..."

"So you didn't love my mother?"

"I cared for her at the time..."

"So you were just fucking?" Chandler just sat there quiet, listening intently...

"No Starr... I gave your mother a job... I gave Wayne a job... I trusted them... and they stole from me..."

"They stole from you?"

"Starr... between the two of them... they stole over $50,000..."

"Mommy told me Wayne set her up..."

"Maybe he did... but $50,000 is a lot of money Starr... somebody had to pay for stealing from me..."

"What about me Daddy?"

"Starr... they didn't think about you when they stole from me..."

"Did you think about me Daddy?"

"Always..."

"But you let my mother sit it jail..."

"I let your mother pay for what she did... I promised her I wouldn't tell Wayne he wasn't your father... I gave up my only daughter... I risked my marriage... and she betrayed me..." my father said as he started to cry...

"Please don't cry Daddy..." I said as I hugged my father...

"My wife doesn't know about you... my wife was in prison with your mother and I still kept my promise to your mother..."

"I'm sorry Daddy..."

"You have nothing to be sorry for..."

"Are you going to tell your wife about me?"

"Of course..."

"I can't wait to meet her..."

"Bazil..." Chandler interrupted...

"Yes Chandler..."

"I need to ask you something...

"Okay..."

"Bazil..."

"Yes Chandler..."

"I'm in love with your daughter..."

"I know..."

"Bazil... listen..."

"Okay..."

"Bazil... I want to marry your daughter..."

"What?" my father and I both said in unison...

"I want to marry your daughter... If you'll give me your blessing..."

"Chandler..." my father whispered as we both started crying...

"Bazil..." Chandler asked as he started to cry... "May I have your blessing to ask your daughter for her hand... in marriage?"

"Yes Chandler... you have my blessing..."

"Starr..."

"Yes Chandler?"

"Stand up..."

"Okay..." I cried as I stood up. Chandler stood up, came close to me, kissed me, and then got down on bended knee...

"Starr..." he said as he opened the ring box... "Will you marry me?"

"Yes Chandler... yes..." Chandler put the ring on my finger, stood up, and pulled me into a kiss. We were kissing so profusely we didn't notice my father easing out the door...

"God... please... How am I going to tell Beautiee?" Bazil asked as he started the car...

"Just tell her the truth..." God answered...

"God... I'm scared... please help me..."

"I'll help you Bazil... I'll always help you... but you're going to have to brace yourself..." Bazil drove the rest of the way in silence. When he got home, he parked the car, went inside, went upstairs, and went into the bedroom...

"Thank God you're asleep..." Bazil whispered...

"You welcome..." God said.

Chapter 10

"Good morning..." Bazil said as he kissed Beautiee awake..."

"Mmmm... good morning..." Beautiee said as she pulled him into a kiss...

"You still want more?" Bazil breathed as he started kissing her neck..."

"Yesss..." she breathed... and then she jumped up out of bed and ran to the bathroom...

"Beautiee... are you alright?"

"Yes..." Beautiee lied...

"I'm coming in there..." Bazil said as he jumped up out of bed and went into the bathroom... "You're throwing up... are you sick?"

"No... I'm just nauseous... must've been something I ate last night..." she lied...

"You sure you're okay?"

"Yes Bazil... I'm fine..." she lied...

"I'll stay here with you..."

"No Bazil... I have to use the bathroom..."

"Okay – when you come out... we need to talk..."

"Is this about last night?" Beautiee asked as she took the pregnancy test out of the back of the bathroom cabinet...

"Yes..."

"Okay... I'll be out in a minute..." she said as she hurried to open the pregnancy test...

"You want some coffee?"

"Yes... that sounds good..." she breathed...

"Okay – I'll go downstairs and make some..." Bazil said as he headed downstairs to the kitchen...

"Oh thank God..." Beautiee breathed as she started to pee...

"You're welcome..." God said...

"Oh my God... I'm pregnant!"

"Beautiee... you comin' down?"

"Yes Bazil... I'm on my way..." she said as she got up, flushed, washed her hands, got dressed, and headed downstairs to the kitchen...

"Beautiee... we need to talk..."

"Yes we do..." Beautiee smiled. She couldn't wait to tell him...

"Beautiee..." Bazil said as tears fell down his cheeks...

"Bazil... what's wrong?" Beautiee said as she sat at the table. She watched Bazil make coffee as tears fell down his cheeks... and she was scared to death. Bazil put the coffee pot on, put the water in the Keurig, and sat down at the table...

"Beautiee... please... don't hate me..." he whispered as he took her hands and held them as he cried...

"Bazil... tell me..."

"I have a daughter... and she needs my help..."

"What the fuck did you just say?" she asked as she snatched her hands away from him and stood up...

"I have a daughter... and she needs my help..."

"Aaaaggghhhh!" Beautiee screamed as she threw the table up with both hands and Bazil had to jump out the way to keep the table from slamming down on his feet...

"Oh Shit – Troy – something's wrong with Beautiee – I'm goin' over there..." Keisha said as she jumped up outta bed...

"Keisha – wait a damn minute!" Troy yelled...

"Troy – remember what happened the last time we waited?"

"You're right – I'm comin' with you – let's go!" Troy said as he jumped up outta bed. They ran downstairs, ran out their house, and made a beeline over to Bazil's...

"Beautiee... wait... let me explain..."

"Explain what mutha fucka?"" she yelled as she picked up the Keurig and threw it on the kitchen floor. The hot water burned Bazil but she didn't give a fuck..."

"Aaah Shit! You burned me!"

"Open the door!" Keisha yelled as she banged on the door but Beautiee ignored her...

"You burned your damn self!" she yelled as she knocked the glasses on the floor and they crashed near Bazil's feet...

"Beautiee! Please! Let me explain!"

"How long have you know you had a daughter?" Beautiee yelled...

"Oh shit – Troy – you hear this?" Keisha whispered..."
"Damn... what the fuck is wrong with him?" Troy asked as they both continued to listen...

"I've always known it was a possibility..."
"What? What the fuck do you mean you've always known it was a possibility? How old is she?" Bazil didn't answer her right away... "Well? How old is she?"
"She's 22..." Bazil sighed...
"Why Bazil? I died for you – I followed you to God – I begged God to let you live – you promised God you'd never hurt me again – you promised me you'd never hurt me again – and you're hurting me again – whhhyyyy?" she screamed...
"I promised her mother..." Bam! It happened so fast she didn't remember doing it – but she did it – she punched Bazil in his fuckin' mouth – and he hit the floor – and he fell right into that pile of broken glass... "Aaahhhh!" Bazil yelled as he hit the floor...

"Oh shit – Keisha – move!" Troy yelled as he broke their front door...

"You lied to me after everything I've been through for you – because of a fuckin' promise you made to another Bitch? Are you fuckin' kidding me? What about your promise to God? What about your promise to me?"

"Oh Shit – Bazil... you alright?" Troy asked as he picked Bazil up off the floor...

"Beautiee... calm down..." Keisha said as she came into the kitchen...

"Ya know what? Right now I'm not sure I want this baby – or this marriage" she screamed as she took her rings off and threw them at Bazil...

"Oh my God... Beautiee... you're pregnant?" Bazil asked as he started to go towards her..."

"Not for long!" she said between gritted teeth... "Keisha – come with me to the doctor – please..." she said as she headed towards the door...

"Alright – I swear to God – you get on my fuckin' nerves Bazil..." she said as she followed Beautiee outside...

"Damn Bazil – what the fuck!" Troy said as he helped Bazil clean up the broken glass...

"I can't help it... I keep fuckin' up – and now she's getting rid of the baby..." Bazil said as he broke down crying...

"Beautiee... wait..."

"Fuck him Keisha – I'm not bringing my child into this drama!" she cried...

"Beautiee... wait a minute... please..." she said as she pulled her into a hug...

"I can't wait Keisha – my stomach is cramping..."

"Oh shit – okay – let's go – we'll take my car..." she said as Beautiee followed her to her car...

"What the fuck happened Bazil?" Troy asked...

"I have a daughter... and she needs my help..."

"Bazil! How old is she?"

"She's 22 years old..."

"Now I see why she knocked the shit outta your ass – I don't know what the fuck is wrong with you Bazil – why didn't you tell her about your daughter?"

"Because I promised her mother I wouldn't tell anyone I was her father..."

"Wait a minute... you promised her mother?"

"Yea – you remember Janet?"

"Yea Bazil – what's Janet got to do with this?"

"Her mother is Janet's best friend..."

"I can't – here..." Troy said as he handed Bazil Beautiee's rings... "Take these – pray to God your wife still wants to be your wife – and put these back on her finger – and go change your shirt – you got blood all over it..." he said as he looked at Bazil in disgust...

"Will you stay here? Bazil asked...

"I'ma stay here until I here from my wife — and I'm not paying for that fuckin' door either..."

"Okay — I'll be back in a minute..." Bazil said as he went upstairs to the bedroom...

"Please God..." Bazil cried as he fell to his knees... "I didn't mean to break my promise to you... I'm sorry..." he said as he broke down crying...

"You sure are sorry..." God said...

"I tried... I really tried..." Bazil cried...

"All you had to do was tell the truth Bazil... it's not hard..."

"I know... please don't let her leave me..."

"That's her choice... it's always been her choice..."

"Please..." Bazil cried...

"I love you... I forgive you... but you need to go to your wife..."

"Please God... touch her heart so she'll forgive me..."

"As long as she has faith in me I'll always touch her heart... but it's her choice to forgive you..."

"Please God... don't let her get rid of my baby..." Bazil cried...

"If I could do that... I would... but you know I can't do that..."

"Please God... help me..."

"I'll always help you Bazil... but right now... you need to help yourself... your wife needs you..."

"She doesn't want me..."

"BAZIL J. OSGOOD!"

"Yes God?"

"I SAID YOUR WIFE NEEDS YOU! NOW!" Bazil got up off is knees, went into the bathroom, and looked at himself in the mirror...

"Oh shit – I need to change – damn!" he said as he took off his shirt and saw he had cuts and bruises all over his body. Bazil put on another shirt and went downstairs...

"Beautiee – take deep breaths... try to relax..." Keisha said as she started driving... "Where's your doctor?"

"She's in Purchase, New York..."

"Why don't you have a doctor up here?"

"She's been my doctor since I was a virgin..." I laughed...

"Oh damn – and she's still delivering babies?"

"Not anymore – now that I'm pregnant I'll have to find another doctor..."

"So how do you get there – you have directions?"

"As soon as you hit Portchester – go down Westchester Avenue – she's the first building – West Med..."

"Oh okay... try to relax..."

"Okay..."

"Now – what happened?"

"I took a pregnancy test..."

"Okay..."

"I was happy..." I said as I started crying...

"Calm down Beautiee..." Keisha said as she rubbed her hand...

"I wanted to tell Bazil... but he said we need to talk... and he started cryin'...

"The fuck he cryin' for?"

"Exactly!"

"What happened?"

"He tells me he has a daughter... and she needs his help..."

"I heard that – but I don't understand – why are you so upset?"

"She's 22 years old Keisha!"

"Wait a minute – he knew?"

"He said he's always known it was a possibility he had a daughter..."

"Now I get it – I'd be upset too..."

"I love him so much Keisha – why does he keep hurting me?" Beautiee cried...

"Girl I'on know... try to stay calm..." she said as she continued rubbing Beautiee's hand...

"Lord... please help me..." Beautiee prayed out loud...

"I was just waiting for you to ask..." God said as he slowed down her heart beat and her blood pressure started to return to normal...

"Did you mean what you said?" Keisha asked...

"I said a lot..." Beautiee laughed...

"About not being pregnant for long..."

"I was hurt..."

"I know..."

"What would you do?"

"You want me to be honest?"

"No... never mind..."

"Let me just say this..."

"Okay..."

"You're pregnant – your hormones are all over the place – don't make a decision today – wait until you've had a chance to calm down..."

"Okay..."

"We're here..." Keisha said as she parked the car..."

"I'm gonna go upstairs... I'll be on the 2nd floor – Dr. Julianne..."

"Okay – I'll be right up..." Keisha said as she took her cell phone out her pocket and read the following text message... "We're right behind you..."

"Oh thank God!" Keisha said out loud as Troy pulled in with Bazil, he parked the car, and they both got out...

"You're welcome..." God said...

"Hey Keisha..." Bazil said...

"Don't speak to me Bazil..."

"Keisha – she alright?" Troy asked...

"She was calm..."

"Where is she?" Bazil asked...

"Troy – check your friend..."

"Bazil – here – take my keys – go sit in the car..." Troy said...

"Aaight..." Bazil said as he took the keys from Troy and went to sit in the car...

"Where is she?" Troy asked...

"She's upstairs on the 2nd floor – Dr. Julianne..."

"You goin' up there?"

"Yea..."

"Aaight – I'ma go sit in the car with Bazil..."

"Good – I'on wanna see his ass right now anyway..." Keisha said as she went inside, got in the elevator, and went to the 2nd floor...

"Do you have an appointment?"

"No..." Beautiee answered as Keisha came inside...

"Do you have an emergency?"

"Yes...."

"What's your emergency?"

"My stomach's cramping..."

"Are you pregnant?"

"Yes..."

"How far along are you?"

"I don't know..."

"Okay... have a seat..." Dawn said as she went to the back...

"You still calm – right?" Keisha asked as she held Beautiee's hand...

"Yea..."

"Beautiee – come with me..." Dawn said as she held the door for her...

"Can she come with me?" Beautiee asked...

"Sure..." Dawn said...

"C'mon Keisha..." Beautiee said as they went down the hall to another room...

"Okay – everything off from the waist down – Dr. Julianne will be here in a few minutes..." she said as she left the room. Beautiee took everything off from the bottom down but her socks and hopped up on the table...

"They don't have any gowns?" Keisha asked...

"Yea... over there..." Beautiee said as she pointed to the pile of gowns...

"Beautiee... your husband's here – can he come in?" Beautiee looked at Keisha and she rolled her eyes...

"Yea..."

"I'on wanna be in here with him – I'm goin' back in the waiting room..." Keisha said as Bazil came in and Keisha went out...

"Beautiee... I'm sorry..." Bazil cried as he went over to Beautiee and laid his head on her stomach...

"Aww... that's a picture..." Dr. Julianne said as she came in the door, took out her cell phone, and took the picture. "You look like you've been crying..."

"I have..." Beautiee said...

"Oh my God – what's wrong? Beautiee... are you okay?"

"I hope so..."

"Let me do a sonogram – Dawn said you're pregnant – and your stomach's cramping... how far along are you?"

"I don't know..." Beautiee said with tears in her eyes..."

"Okay – try to relax – let's have a look..." she said as she went between Beautiee's legs... "Oh dear... you have some spotting... let me do a sonogram... hand me that gel..." she said, pointing to the gel. Bazil handed her the gel, she squeezed some gel onto Beautiee's stomach, and turned on the machine. "Oh my goodness – I'd say you're about 3 to 4 months – look at your baby..." she said as she kept moving the sensor across her stomach. Bazil and Beautiee looked at their baby on the screen and he took her hand. "She's a busy lil' thing..." Dr. Julianne said as they watched their baby moving around...

"She?" Bazil asked...

"Don't mind me – I think all babies are girls..." she laughed... "Everything seems okay – but I want you to stay here for another hour or so to make sure you stop spotting – did you lift something heavy?"

"Yea..." Beautiee answered...

"Why would you do that when you know you're pregnant?"

"I was angry... so I threw the table over..."

"Beautiee – you can't go throwing tables – even if you're not pregnant – what the hell happened?"

"It's my fault Dr. Julianne..." Bazil said...

"Look – I don't know what's going on between you two – but if you want a healthy baby you need to knock it off! Beautiee – can I speak to you in private?"

"Yea..."

"Mr. Osgood – go wait outside..."

"Okay..." Bazil said as he left the room and closed the door...

"Beautiee – are you in trouble?"

"No..."

"Did he hurt you?"

"No..."

"What happened?"

"He told me he has a daughter... with someone else..." she said as she started crying...

"Oh Beautiee!" I'm sorry... c'mere..." she said as she pulled Beautiee into a hug...

"I told him I wasn't sure I wanted his baby... but I didn't mean it... I was just hurt..."

"Is that why you threw the table?"

"Yea..."

"So... you're keeping the baby?"

"Yea..."

"Oh thank God!" she breathed...

"You're welcome..." God said...

"I want you to go back in the waiting room... I'm gonna check you again in about an hour... I wanna make sure you don't have any more spotting..."

"Okay..." Beautiee said as she hopped down off the table and got dressed...

"I'll see you in a while – I gotta get to my next patient..." she said as she left the room and Beautiee went back into the waiting area...

"Hey..." Keisha said as Beautiee sat next to her... "You alright?"

"She wants me to wait about an hour... then she's going to check me again to make sure..."

"So you're having a baby?"

"Yea..." she smiled as Bazil took Beautiee's hand and kissed it...

"Thank God!" Keisha said...

"You're welcome!" God said...

"Yo – they have a cafeteria in here?" Troy asked...

"As a matter-of-fact – they do – and they make good food..."

"Let's go" Troy said as he got up...

"Dawn – I'll be back – we're going to eat..." Beautiee said...

"Okay Beautiee – see you soon..." We all went to the elevator and took it to the cafeteria. When we got to the table, Troy got impatient...

"What we gettin'?"

"Cheese steak and fries..." Beautiee answered... "Bazil – give them your card..."

"Okay..." Keisha and Troy went to place the order and then Beautiee spoke...

"Tell me about your daughter..."

"Her name is Starr..."

"You said you've always known there was a possibility... are you sure?"

"She looks just like me..."

"Okay..."

"When I was married to Janet..."

"Go ahead Bazil... tell me..."

"I'm scared you're going to throw another table..." he laughed...

"C'mon Keisha – let's go sit over by the window so they can talk..."

"Aaight..."

"When I was married to Janet... I slept with her best friend..."

"Okay... " Beautiee sighed...

"Her name is Mary..."

"Wait a minute... Mary?"

"Yea..."

"Mary Smith?"

"Yes..."

"You mean to tell me... I was in prison... with your Baby Momma?"

"Yes..."

"So... you promised your Baby Momma..."

"Beautiee... please... let me explain..."

"Okay Bazil..."

"When Mary got pregnant... she was seeing someone else... she begged me not to tell him because he wanted children... he worked for me at the time... and so did she..."

"So you agreed..."

"Yes..."

"Did you ever get a DNA test?"

"No..."

"Okay... so what happened?"

"Mary got arrested for embezzlement... she begged me not to prosecute... she said he set her up... but it was over $50,000... that was a lot of money... I was angry – I didn't give a damn who paid for the crime..."

"What about your daughter?"

"Wayne raised her up until she was 18... and then he left her to fend for herself..."

"You never went to see about her?"

"It was never an issue... until now..."

"Why is it an issue now?'

"Wayne always wanted children... he was a good father... but since she turned 18... he left... she has an apartment... she has Section 8... but she doesn't have a job right now... she's struggling to make ends meet... her mother's up for parole... her mother can't stay in Section 8 housing because she has a felony... if Starr takes her mother in she'll forfeit her Section 8 and they'll be homeless..." he explained with tears in his eyes...

"All you had to do was tell me the truth Bazil – you shouldn't have kept this from me..."

"I know... I'm sorry..."

"Bazil?"

"Yes?"

"How do you know all this?"

"My daughter is dating Chandler..."

"Chandler? Sergeant Chandler?"

"Yea..."

"Oh hell no – Keisha – Troy – y'all gotta here this!" Beautiee laughed...

"Here – eat!" Troy said as he brought our food to us...

"Thank you – I was hungry!" Beautiee said as she snatched up the steak and cheese sandwich and started eating...

"Okay – what's going on?" Keisha asked as she sat down...

"Girl!" Beautiee laughed between bites... "Her name is Starr – and she's dating Chandler! Haa Haa!" Bazil just ate without saying a word...

"Chandler? Sergeant Chandler? Damn! How old is she again?"

"She's twenty twooooo!" Beautiee blurted...

"How the... never mind... I can't..."

"We need to get back upstairs..." Bazil said...

"Le'me finish this first..." Beautiee said as she took the last bite... "Okay – let's go y'all..." Beautiee said as she got up from the table... "Oh shoot – I got a message – let me see who's texting me..." she said as she pulled out her cell phone...

"Beautiee... you okay? Why you cryin'?" Keisha asked as she put her arm around Beautiee...

"We're having a baby..." Beautiee whispered as she showed Keisha the picture of Bazil lying on her stomach. In the background you could see the sonogram machine and their baby on the screen...

"Aww... Troy... look..." Keisha said as she showed Troy the picture. Troy looked at the picture and passed the phone to Bazil. Bazil looked at the picture and started crying...

"C'mon – get in already!" Keisha laughed as we all got in the elevator. When we got to Dr. Julianne's office, Dawn was waiting...

"Let's go Beautiee..." Dawn said as Bazil followed. Keisha and Troy sat down in the waiting room. When Beautiee got in the room and stripped down again, she hopped up on the table.

"Pass me a gown Bazil..." she said.

"Here ya go..." Bazil said as Dr. Julianne came into the room...

"Okay Beautiee... let's see what's going on down here..." she said as she went between

Beautiee's legs... "Do you mind?" Dr. Julianne asked as Bazil loomed over her shoulder...

"Sorry..."

"You can look... just don't breathe down my damn neck!" she laughed... "Okay Beautiee – I need to examine you..." she said as she squirted some gel on her hand before inserting her fingers... "Any tenderness? She asked...

"A little..."

"Okay – I don't see anything..." she said as she pulled her fingers out and took off the glove... you can get dressed... I'll be right back... she said as she left the room...

"Whew!" Thank God!" Beautiee said...

"Yes... Thank God!" Bazil said...

"You're welcome!" God said. Beautiee got dressed and waited for Dr. Julianne...

"Okay Beautiee – you can go..."

"Thank you..." Beautiee said as she hopped down off the table...

"Mr. Osgood?"

"Yes Dr. Julianne?"

"I need to speak to you in private..." Beautiee smiled as she left the room because she knew what was coming next... "Le'me tell you something mutha fucka..." she said as she grabbed Bazil by the collar... "I don't play when it comes to my patients – if you ever do anything else to upset her, hurt her, make her cry, or cause her to miscarry – I'll hurt you – violently – and I don't throw tables – I throw men – do you understand me?"

"Yes Dr. Julianne..."

"Good..." she said as she adjusted his shirt... "Now go home – love your wife – love her pussy – and love your baby..."

"Did you just tell me to love her pussy?"

"You've never had pregnant pussy before have you?"

"No..."

"You're in for a wild ride... she's twelve weeks pregnant – her hormones are on 10 – she's gonna want – and need – your dick..."

"Is that right?"

"That's right..."

"Dr. Julianne?"

"Yes Mr. Osgood?"

"How long can we have sex?"

"You can fuck up 'till it's time to deliver if she wants... and she will..." she laughed...

"Are you sure?"

"Trust me... I know my patients..." she said as she left the room...

"Y'all ready?" Keisha asked...

"Yea... we ready..." Bazil laughed...

"Y'all good?" Troy asked...

"Yea... we're good..." Beautiee sighed...

"Good – let's go..." Keisha said...

"Thank you Keisha..." Bazil said as he kissed her on the cheek...

"Troy – check your friend..." she said as we all laughed and went to the elevator.

Chapter 11

When they got home, Bazil pulled Beautiee close to him and kissed her...

"Mmmm..." Beautiee breathed...

"I love you so much..." Bazil said...

"I love you too..." Beautiee said...

"Come with me..." Bazil said as he took her hand, led her upstairs, and into the bedroom...

"Oh Bazil..." she whispered as 'Forever Mine' started playing...

"Forever Mine..." Bazil sang as he pulled her close to him and they began dancing... "All because..." he sang as he kissed her neck... "You're my kind..." and she started to cry.... "I got what you want, you got what I want... and we were made... for each other..." he sang... and then he kissed her...

"Forever Mine..." he sang and then he kissed her again... "And I'm so glad 'cause it gets better with time..." he said as he moved his hands up and down her back... "I like what you like, you like what I like... and we were made for each other..." he sang...

"Listen Beautiee... you are someone that I've been hoping, I've been lookin' all my days..." he sang... "Don't you ever think about leaving..." he said in between kisses... "My heart would be grievin'...

"Forever Mine..." he sang as he started to undress her... "Ah, we're one of a kind..." he sang as he removed all her clothes... "Mmmm... I need what you need... you need what I need... and we were made for each other..." he sang as he began to undress... "Oh baby... I wanna love, love you so, make it good right down to the bone, to the bone..." he sang as he removed all his clothes... ""Cause it's you I'm thinkin' about pleasin'" he sang as he led her to the bed... "Give you all the love you're needin'" he sang as he pushed her down on her back... "Don't go, please stay stay..." he sang as he spread her legs...

"Forever Mine..." he sang as he began kissing her up her body... ""Cause..." he sang as he kissed her stomach... "We get along just fine... I got what you want... Good lovin'..." he sang as he thrust himself inside her... "You got what I want... Good lovin'" he sang as he continued thrusting... and we were made for each other...

"Bazil..." she moaned... "Yes... Beautiee..." he breathed as he put her arms up and clasped his hands with hers before putting his tongue in her mouth...

"Mmmmm... Mmmmm... Mmmmm.... Mmmmm..." she moaned in his mouth as she wrapped her legs around his back, pulling him in deeper...

"Yes Beautiee..." he breathed... "That's it... let me love you..." he said as he held her and kissed her neck, her shoulders, and then put his tongue back in her mouth, kissing her harder, thrusting harder...

"Mmmmm! Mmmmm! Mmmmm! Mmmmm!" she moaned as her orgasm was climbing...

"Mmmph! Mmmph! Mmmph! Mmmph!" Bazil moaned back in her mouth...

"Bazil... Fuck me... I'm cumming!" she screamed as her orgasm traveled up her arms to her hands, and back down her body...

"Yes Beautiee... cum for me..."

"Bazil! Don't stop – I'm cumming again... Aaaggghhhh!" Bazil held her and fucked her hard as her body began to tremble...

"Fuck... I'm cumming with you... Uggghh! Ugghh! Ugghh! Ugghh! Uuugggghhhh!" Bazil slowed down but didn't stop... "Damn... that was so fucking good..." Beautiee breathed...

"Yes Beautiee... it was..."

"I needed that..." she breathed...

"Yes... you did..." he said and then he kissed her again...

"I love you... My Thirst Quencher..."

"Beautiee?"

"Yes... My Thirst Quencher..."

"You know I'll never let you leave me... right?"

"Yes... My Thirst Quencher..."

"You know I have to punish you... right?"

"Yes... My Thirst Quencher..."

"Mmmm... Good..." he said as he put his tongue in her mouth and started kissing her hard...

"Wait..." she breathed as she pushed him up a bit...

"No..." Bazil breathed...

"I need..."

"You... need... to..." he interrupted as he started thrusting... "Let... me... do... what... Dr. Julianne... told... me... to... do..."

"Ooohhh.... What's that?" she moaned...

"She... told... me... to... love... you..." he said and then he kissed her... "Love... your... pussy..." he said and then he kissed her again... "And... love... our... baby..."

"Ooohhh.... Bazil..."

"Yes... Beautiee..."

"Don't stop..." she moaned...

"Who... am... I?"

"My... Thirst... Quencher..."

"Who's... pusssy... is... this?" he asked as he began pounding her pussy..."

"Yooouuurrsss!" she moaned...

"Who's... fuckin... you?"

"You are..."

"Say it..."

"Ohhhh... Bazil..." she moaned...

"Say it!"

"Fuck Me! Oh God! I'm cumming!" she screamed...

"Uggghh! Ugghh! Ugghh! Ugghh! Uuugggghhhh!" Bazil collapsed on top of her and smothered her with his mouth as he kissed her hard and deep. Beautiee was in euphoric heaven...

"Shit..." she breathed... "Is this what I have to look forward to?"

"According to Dr. Julianne..." he said as he kissed her again... "Yes..."

"Mmmm.... Thank you baby girl..." she breathed...

"Yes... Thank you baby girl..." Bazil breathed. They continued to lay together kissing for a few moments, and then Bazil spoke... "We need to talk..." he said as he got up off the bed...

"Okay..." Beautiee said as she got up. Bazil got his robe, put it on, brought Beautiee her robe, and sat down as she put her robe on.

"Sit here..." he said as he patted the bed and she sat beside him. "A lot happened today..."

"Yes it did..." I said as Bazil started to cry... "Please don't cry Bazil..."

"I'm sorry I hurt you... I didn't mean to..."

"I know Bazil..." Beautiee said as she wiped his tears. Bazil stood up, opened his robe, and showed Beautiee the cuts and bruises on his body from the broken glass, and Beautiee started crying too...

"This can heal..." Bazil said... "But do you see these?" he asked as he took her rings out his pocket...

"Yes Bazil..."

"When you took these off... and threw them... you broke my heart..." Bazil said as he sat back down next to her and broke down crying..."

"I'm sorry..." Beautiee whispered as she pulled him into a hug, held him, and cried with him...

"Promise me... no matter what happens... you'll never break my heart again..."

"I promise..." she said as she kissed him... "I'll never break your heart again..."

"Do you mean that?"

"Yes... My Thirst Quencher... I'll never break your heart again... I promise..."

"Okay... now..." he said as he took her hand... "I'm going to put these back on your finger... and I don't ever want you to take them off again... do you understand me?"

"Yes..."

"Okay..." he said as he put them back on her finger... "Now... I need to talk... and I need you to listen..." he said as he took her hands...

"Okay..."

"I want to help my daughter..."

"Okay..."

"I want us to be in her life..."

"Okay..."

"Is that okay with you?"

"Of course that's okay with me..."

"Really?"

"Yes..." Beautiee said as she pulled him into a kiss... "I can't wait for her to meet her little sister..."

"A girl?"

"I think so..." Beautiee smiled...

"Beautiee?"

"Yes Bazil?"

"What's gonna happen if I find out I have another child somewhere?"

"Bazil?"

"Yes Beautiee?"

"I need you to promise me something..."

"Okay..."

"I need you to promise me - no matter what it is — that you'll tell me as soon as you find out..."

"What if I have another 22 year old? Are you going to throw another table? Are you going to throw another coffee pot?"

"Bazil — I didn't throw those things and break the glasses because you have a daughter — I threw those things and broke the glasses because you knew — I was in jail with your baby momma and you knew — and you didn't tell me — where you ever gonna tell me?"

"I was scared to tell you — you went through so much..."

"What if she knocked on the door one day and I answered the door?"

"You're right..." he said as he took Beautiee's hands... "I promise — I'll never do that to you again..."

"Do you mean that Bazil?"

121

"Yes Beautiee... I promise..."

"Is this a promise you can keep Bazil?"

"Yes Beautiee... it's a promise I can keep..."

"Okay – I need to ask you something..."

"Okay..."

"Are you sure this is your daughter?"

"Yes..."

"How are you sure?"

"They have my DNA from when I was in prison – they have Starr's DNA in the system – Chandler told me it's a match..."

"Why do they have her DNA?"

"When she went to apply for Section 8, she had to go to DSS to do a drug & alcohol assessment to qualify..."

"Have you seen her?"

"Yes..."

"When?"

"I saw her last night."

"Where?"

"At Chandler's place."

"Did you know she was going to be there?"

"No..."

"What happened?"

"A lot..."

"Tell me..."

"We held each other and cried..."

"So she was happy to see you..."

"Yes..."

"Did you talk about her mother?"

"We talked about everything..."

"How did she take it?"

"It was hard..."

"Hard for her? Or hard for you?"

"Hard for both of us... but especially me..."

"Why? What happened?"

"I told her everything Mary didn't..."

"What did you tell her?"

"Please don't hate me..."

"I couldn't hate you if I wanted to..."

"You promise?"

"I promise..."

"I told her I cared about her mother... but I was in love with my wife..."

"Janet..."

"Yes..."

"She said she understood why her mother hates me..."

"She has no business hating you..."

"Yes she does..."

"Why?"

"Because she was in love with me... and I knew it... and I fucked' her anyway..."

"You didn't tell Starr that... did you?"

"I told Starr that I cared for her mother, I gave her mother and Wayne a job, I gave up my only daughter,... and... even after they betrayed me... I still kept my promise to her mother... and I kept it all... from you..." Bazil said as he started to cry..." Beautiee didn't say anything – she just pulled Bazil into a hug, held him, and let him cry on her shoulder for a few moments...

"Was Chandler there?"

"Yes..."

"What did Chandler say?"

"He didn't say anything about that... but..."

"What Bazil? What happened?"

"Chandler started to cry..."

"Oh my God... Bazil..."

"He told me he was in love with my daughter...

"Aww..."

"And he told me he wanted to marry my daughter..."

"Wow... that's beautiful..."

"He asked me if I would give him my blessing... and I said yes..."

"Oh Bazil..." Beautiee said with tears in her eyes..."

"And then he asked Starr to stand up... and he got down on bended knee... and he proposed..."

"Bazil..."

"It was the most beautiful moment..."

"I bet..."

"I knocked the shit out of him earlier... at the restaurant..."

"I know you did..."

"How do you know?"

"I know you very well Bazil..."

"Yes you do..."

"You thought he was taking advantage of your daughter..."

"And now he's going to marry her..."

"So she said yes?"

"Yes... she said yes..."

"We have a lot to celebrate..."

124

"Yes we do..."

"We're going to have a bridal party, a wedding, and a baby shower..." Beautiee sighed...

"I love you so much Beautiee..."

"I love you too..."

"I have her picture..."

"Show me..."

"Here..." Bazil said as he took his phone out his pocket and showed Beautiee her picture...

"Oh my God! She's beautiful!"

"And Chandler is in love with her... just like I'm in love with you..." he said as he pushed Beautiee down on the bed and kissed her...

"Wait a minute..." Beautiee laughed...

"What's so funny?"

"Sergeant Chandler... is going to be your son in law!"

"You're right... that is funny..." Bazil laughed as they held each other and continued kissing...

Chapter 12

"Hello?" I said as I answered my phone...

"You have a collect call from an inmate at the Bridgeport Correctional Facility – will you accept the call?"

"Yes I will..."

"Hey Starr..."

"Hey Mommy! I'm so excited..." I exclaimed as I kept looking out the window...

"What's going on?"

"Daddy's on his way to come get me..."

"Starr – I know you're excited – but I don't want you to get your hopes up..."

"Why Mommy? I thought you said she was nice..."

"She was nice – but she didn't know I had a baby with her husband..."

"Why didn't you tell her?"

"Once I found out she was married to your father I steered clear of her..."

"Why Mommy?"

"I didn't think it was my place – that should've come from her husband..."

"Maybe he told her Mommy..."

"Trust me – if she knew I had a baby with her husband – she wouldn't have been so nice to me..."

"Why was she in jail anyway?"

"I really shouldn't discuss that with you Starr..."

"What if I google it?"

"What you find out in google is between you and google..."

"So you're not going to tell me?"

"No... it's not my business..."

"Okay – oh shoot – Daddy's downstairs – bye Mommy!" I said as I hung up the phone, ran out the door, and ran down the stairs... "Daddy!"

"I guess you're happy to see me..." my father laughed...

"I can't wait to meet your wife – Mommy says she's really nice..." I said as I got in the car...

"That was nice of her to say..."

"Daddy?"

"Yes Starr?"

"Can I ask you a question?"

"Sure..."

"Mommy says Beautiee was in jail with her..."

"She was..."

"Can you tell me why?"

"Sigh... she was in jail for trying to kill me..."

"Oh my God! She tried to kill you? Why?"

"Starr..."

"Why Daddy?"

"Starr... let it go..." I didn't want to let it go but I saw the look on my father's face change... and he looked sad...

"Okay Daddy..." We didn't talk anymore. I looked out the window as my father drove to Milford, Connecticut. "Ooohhh... you have a Golden Corral..."

"You like Golden Corral?"

"Yea..."

"We can go there... if you want..."

"I'd like that..." I said as we turned the corner and went a few more blocks...

"We're here..." he said as we pulled into the driveway of 54 Maple Street.

"I'm really nervous..."

"Don't be..." he said as he opened the door and I followed him inside... "Beautiee... where are you?"

"In the kitchen..." I followed my dad into the kitchen and watched him go to his wife... "Beautiee... this is my daughter... Starr..." I was relieved when she started smiling...

"You're even more beautiful in person..." she said as she hugged me...

"Thank you... nice meeting you too... can I ask you a question?"

"Sure..."

"Are you pregnant?" Beautiee looked at my father and smiled...

"You told her didn't you?"

"Actually – I didn't..."

"How'd you know I was pregnant Starr?"

"I felt it..."

"Ohh... you're a sensitive..."

"A sensitive?"

"Yes – a sensitive is a person that's in tune to what's going on around them – you feel more than anyone else..."

"My mom says that..."

"I made coffee – you want some?"

"Sure..."

"Okay..." Beautiee said as she took down three cups and made coffee...

"Ooohhh... this is good..." I said...

"Thank you..."

"Starr wants to go to the Golden Corral..." my father said...

"Sounds good – let's go!" Beautiee said as she ran towards the door...

"Okay then!" my dad laughed as we left the house and got in the car. We didn't have far to go so we were standing in line in a matter of minutes... "I love their breakfast..." Beautiee said...

"I've never tried it..."

"You're in for a treat..."

"Welcome to Golden Corral – how many people are in your party?" the cashier asked...

"Three..." my father answered...

"Would you like coffee with your breakfast?"

"Juice will be fine..."

"Why didn't my dad get coffee?" I asked...

"Their coffee isn't that good..." Beautiee whispered in my ear...

"Oohhh... okay..."

"This way please..." the hostess said as she directed us to our booth.

"Ladies – go ahead – I'll wait until you get back..." my father said...

"C'mon Starr..." Beautiee said as she took my hand and pulled me up from the table...

"Okay..." I laughed. We got our plates and I stood there looking around...

"You okay Starr?" Beautiee asked...

"Yea..."

"You sure?"

"Yea... everything looks so good..."

"Start at this end – just get a little bit of everything – in case you don't like something..."

"Okay..." I said. I followed Beautiee from one buffet to another, taking a little bit of everything from grits, to eggs, to French toast, to home fries, to bacon, to sausage, to ham, and to hush puppies...

"I guess you were a lil' hungry..." my father laughed as we sat down with our plates...

"Go ahead Honey..." Beautiee said... "I'll wait 'till you get back..."

"I won't be long..." my father said as he got up...

"Do I have to wait?" I asked...

"Oh Starr – don't mind me – I was raised by my grandparents – we would all sit at the table and nobody would start eating until everyone was seated..."

"I'll wait too then..." I said...

"Aww... you waited for me..." my father said...

"Yea..." I said...

"Okay – quick grace – Lord bless this food – amen!" Now let's eat!" my father laughed as we ate and started drinking...

"Oohhh... I'm getting full..." I said as I rubbed my stomach..."

"That's why I don't drink while I heat – this way I don't get bloated..." Beautiee said...

"You just want room for all that food on your plate!" my father laughed...

"Well – I guess that doesn't apply to you – you don't have any food left!" Beautiee laughed...

"See..." my father said as he finished his juice... "Unlike you ladies – I didn't sit down at this table to play with my food – I sat down at this table to eat!" my father laughed...

"Well... I can't eat anything else..." I said as I rubbed my stomach...

"I guess you're ready to leave then..." my father said as he got up from the table...

"Yea... I'm ready..."

"I'm ready too..." Beautiee said. We went out to the car and got it...

"So what's the plan for the rest of the day?" I asked...

"You're gonna hang out with us... is that alright?" Beautiee asked...

"That's fine..." I said as I smiled. I didn't ask where we were going – it didn't matter – I was just happy to be with my father...

"We're here..." my father said.

"Were are we?" I asked...

"We're at Osgood Publishing..."

"Osgood Publishing? You have your own publishing company?"

"Yes Starr..."

"What kind of books do you publish?" I asked as we got out the car and went towards the entrance...

"I publish fiction – Beautiee publishes erotic fiction..."

"Oh wow – Beautiee – you write books too?"

"Yes Starr..."

"Can I read them?"

"Sure – let's go inside..." Beautiee said...

"Bazil!" a man said as we come inside...

"Hello Sam..." my father said...

"I thought you were off today?"

"I was – but I wanted everyone to meet my children..."

"Your children?"

"Yes Sam – this is my daughter, Starr... and this is Baby Osgood..." my father said as he rubbed Beautiee's belly...

"Oh wow! Congratulations!"

"Hey y'all..." a woman said as she walked up to us...

"Babe – guess what?" Sam asked...

"Let me tell Joselyn!" Beautiee said...

"Tell me what?"

"These are our children – this is our daughter, Starr... and this is Baby Osgood..." she said as she rubbed her belly..."

"What?! Oh my God – congratulations!" she said as she grabbed Beautiee into a hug...

"Thank you Joselyn..." Beautiee said...

"Nice to meet you Starr – this is my husband and Vice President, Sam Logan..."

"Oh – that's nice..." I said...

"I'm their personal assistant – Beautiee promoted me her first day here..."

"You did?" I asked as I looked at Beautiee...

"I sure did..." Beautiee said as she smiled...

"I thought you were off today..." another woman said as she walked up to us...

"Mommy – you're not going to believe this..." Joselyn said...

"What happened now?" her mother laughed...

"Mommy – this is their daughter, Starr... and this is Baby Osgood..." Joselyn said as she rubbed Beautiee's belly...

"Wow... hi Baby Osgood!" she said as she rubbed Beautiee's belly... "You look just like your father Starr..." her mother said...

"Thank you..." I said...

"Starr – this is my mother and Chief Financial Officer, Sheila Henley..."

"Oh wow – Daddy – you hired the family?"

"I hired Sam first..." my father explained... "Then I hired his wife Joselyn and her mother, Sheila..."

"Maybe one day I can work here too..." I said...

"C'mon – I'll show you around..." my father said as we all followed him into his office...

"This is where I sit – that side belongs to Beautiee..."

"Aww... that's nice – you get to be with Daddy all day..."

"Yes it is nice – especially since Joselyn had our office re-designed..." Beautiee said...

"She did?" I asked...

"When we came back to work, Joselyn called HGTV, told them we were newlyweds, and David Bromstad fell in love with our story...

"David Bromstad? From Color Splash?"

"Oh so you know who he is too..." Joselyn laughed...

"You must really love my father..."

"I do – and I love Mrs. Osgood too!"

"Mrs. Osgood? Do I have to call you that Beautiee?"

"No Starr – they call me Mrs. Osgood because I'm their boss..."

"Ooohhh... okay..."

"C'mon – I'll take you around the office..." Beautiee said as she took me by the arm and we went down the hall...

"Sam?"

"Yes Bazil?"

"Close the door... we need to talk..."

"Okay..." Sam said as he closed the door...

"She can't ever work here Sam..."

"Why not? She's really sweet – she'd be happy to work with her father..."

"She can't ever work here because... she's Mary's daughter..."

"Oh damn!"

"I love my daughter... but I can't go through that after what Mary did to me... after what Wayne did to me..."

"Bazil... I got it..."

"Hey Ladies..." my father said as Beautiee and I walked into the office... "Are you ready?"

"Yes..." Beautiee answered...

"I'll be back next week Sam – take care..." my father said as we left the office. We walked to the car without speaking. After we got in the car I had to say something...

"Daddy?"

"Yes Starr..."

"Are you okay?"

"Yes Starr..."

"You sure?"

"Yes Starr..." I knew he was lying because he wouldn't look at me – he just kept driving....

"Where are we going now?"

"Where would you like to go? Are you ready to go back home?"

"Is that what you want Daddy?"

"Don't be Silly!" my father laughed... "Where would you like to go?"

"Can we go to the movies?"

"Yes we can!" Beautiee answered before my father could say anything...

"I guess we're going to the movies then..." my father laughed...

"We've got the Avengers Endgame at 12:40 and we've got The Intruder at 3:45..." Beautiee said...

"The Intruder doesn't start earlier?" I asked...

"Yes – it starts at 12:55..."

"Why don't we go to that one?" I asked...

"Because I really wanted to see the Avengers – but we can go see The Intruder if you want – long as we're going to the movies – I don't care!" Beautiee laughed...

"Don't I have a say?" my father asked...

"Umm... we'll let you buy the popcorn Daddy!" I laughed...

"Alrighty..." my father laughed as he parked the car and we went into the mall. My father took my hand, Beautiee took his arm, and we went up the escalator. My father was beaming with pride and it made me happy to see him happy. My father got the tickets, got us popcorn, got us soda, and we went into the theatre. Beautiee and I both snuggled up underneath him and we stayed like that through the end of the move. Before we got up to leave I saw Beautiee texting and then I saw my father pull his phone out his pocket and smile.

"She really loves him..." I thought to myself as we left and went to get in the car...

"Sure is quiet in here..." my father laughed...

"I'm just thinking..." Beautiee said...

"Did you enjoy the movie?"

"I know I did..." I said...

"Did you enjoy the movie Beautiee?"

"Yes Bazil... she answered as she drifted off to wherever she was in thought before we interrupted her...

"Where are we going now?" I asked...

"We're going home..." my father answered. I sat there quiet until we got to the house and got out the car...

"Hey Keisha, hey Troy..." Beautiee said as we got up to the front door...

"Hey Beautiee, hey Bazil..." Keisha said. Troy didn't say anything – he just pulled Beautiee into a hug and gave my father a pound...

"This is my daughter, Starr..." my father said as he introduced me...

"Oh my God – she's beautiful... hi Starr..." Troy said as he smiled...

"Hi Troy... it's nice to meet you..." I said...

"You look just like your father..." Keisha said as she hugged me...

"Nice meeting you too Keisha..." I said...

"Let's go inside..." my father said as he opened the door and we went inside... "We're going in the Library for a bit – we'll join you ladies in a few..." my father said as I followed Beautiee and Keisha into the living room and we sat down...

"I heard you're dating Chandler..." Keisha said... "Is it serious?"

"Yes... it is..." I sighed...

"Y'all fuckin'?"

"Damn Keisha!" Beautiee laughed... "She don't know you like that!"

"Well – she might not know me like that – but she goin' learn me – y'all fuckin' or not?" Keisha laughed. I was embarrassed that she was so forward but I didn't want them to see that so I turned the tables...

"Are you?"

"Awww shit!" Beautiee laughed...

"Let me tell you something lil' girl – I've been fuckin' my husband since the first night I met him!" Keisha laughed. I started to realize she didn't mean to put me on the spot but I still wasn't ready to talk about myself yet so I asked her a question...

"You really liked him huh?"

"I did – I just knew – sometimes you know right away..."

"Yea... it was like that for me too..."

"So you slept with Chandler right away?"

"Not right away – but I knew I was going to..."

"Aww..." Keisha said...

"Was it like that for you Beautiee?" I asked...

"Not exactly..."

"I'm sorry..."

"Oh no Starr – that's not what I meant..."

"What was it like?"

"When I met your father – I was in a bad place..."

"Oh wow..."

"At first... I didn't remember what happened to me..."

"Oh my God..."

"Your father came up to me while I was sitting at the bar... I asked him who he was... he said I'm Your Thirst Quencher... and he's been quenching my thirst ever since..."

"I hear that!" Keisha laughed as we high-fived...

"Oh so you had great sex!" I laughed...

"No Starr..."

"Okay – what happened – 'cause I don't get it..."

"Shhh! Listen!" Keisha said...

"Starr..."

"Yes Beautiee?"

"After your father told me he was My Thirst Quencher we shared a drink... and a kiss..."

"Oh... so he was romantic..."

"Yea..." she sighed... "Your father asked me to go to his room with him... I said no... at first... but..."

"You changed your mind?"

"Yea..." she sighed again... "When we got off the elevator I changed my mind again... but your father convinced me to go with him..."

"How'd he do that?"

"He said please don't leave him... and I couldn't..."

"Aww..."

"After we went inside..."

"Okay – stop – I don't need to hear anymore..."

"Girl hush!" Keisha said... "Go 'head Beautiee...

"I told your father I needed to take a shower... so he undressed me... and he saw the bruises..."

"Oh my God! What happened?" I asked...

"He took me into the shower and he was really gentle... and then he cut himself..."

"Oh my God! How did he cut himself?"

"I had glass in my hair..."

"Somebody beat you?"

"Yea..."

"Oh my God... Beautiee... I'm so sorry..." I said as I got up and threw my arms around her...

"Aww... thank you Starr..." she said as she hugged me back... "That's what your father said...

"So Daddy took care of you?"

"Yea... he held me until I fell asleep..." she answered as she smiled...

"Aww... that's beautiful..."

"It was. Your father saved my life... that's why when he asked me to marry him the next day... I said yes..."

"Oh my God! You only knew Daddy for 24 hours? And you said yes?"

"Yea..." she sighed as she smiled...

"Wow... I guess you knew too..."

"Yes... I knew..."

"Wow... I'm just like y'all..." I said as I smiled...

140

"Told ya!" Keisha laughed...

"Beautiee... can I ask you a personal question?"

"Yes Starr – we made love..."

"I wasn't gonna ask you that..."

"Oh... sorry..." she laughed... "What do you wanna know?"

"Did you love Daddy?"

"Yea..."

"Y'all good Bazil?" Troy asked...

"Yea..." Bazil sighed...

"What happened after you got home from the doctor?"

"I sang to her..."

"See – that's what the fuck I'm talkin' about!" Troy yelled as they hugged... "What'd you sing?"

"I sang the beginning of Forever Mine..."

"Aww... damn – that's what's up..."

"And then I performed the rest of the song... on her..."

"Oh shit – I'ma do that to Keisha..."

"I'm the luckiest man in the world..."

"I know that's right – but – real talk – she wasn't leaving you anyway..."

"I was scared... I'd never seen her so hurt... so angry..."

"She's pregnant Bazil..."

"I know..."

"If she wasn't pregnant her emotions wouldn't have been so high..."

"I know..."

"You're done with that right?"

"Oh hell yea!"

"Good – 'cause if my wife cuts you off I gotta cut you off..." Troy laughed...

"I know..." Bazil laughed... "Having Keisha mad at me is worse than having Beautiee mad at me – at least Beautiee loves me..."

"You right – I'm just glad y'all are good..."

"Thank God..."

"You're welcome..." God said...

"Sure is quiet in there – let's go see what they're up to..."

"Okay..." Bazil said as they both came into the living room... "Ladies..." Bazil said as they came into the living room...

"We gotta get going Troy..." Keisha said...

"You sure?" Feels like we just got there..." Troy said...

"We've been here for a little while – but we have some things to do – they ain't goin' nowhere – I'll let you come back!" Keisha laughed...

"Let me?" Troy asked...

"Did I stutter?" Keisha asked as she stood up...

"Stop playin' Keisha..." Troy laughed...

"I'm not playin' wichu... I said..." she said as she walked over to Troy... and he grabbed her... "Stop it!" Keisha laughed as Troy started tickling her...

"You ain't playin'? Huh?" Troy asked as he kept tickling her...

"Stop it... I can't... you gon' make me pee!" she laughed...

"Okay..." Troy said as he stopped but wouldn't let her go...

"Let go of me Troy..."

"Girl..." Troy said as he started kissing Keisha on her neck... "I'll never... ever... let... you... go..."

"Fine then..." Keisha laughed as she started walking towards the front door with Troy holding on to her, still kissing her on her neck...

"I'll... never... ever... let... you... go..."

"Bye y'all..." Keisha laughed as she went out the door, Troy was still holding on, still kissing her on her neck...

"I'll... never... ever... let... you... go..."

"Aww... they're in love..." I sighed...

"Look... he still won't let go..." my father laughed as he looked out the window. Beautiee and I both got up, went to the window, and we could see them, walking down the street, Troy still holding on to her, still kissing her on her neck...

"He'll never, ever let her go..." my father laughed...

"I guess I better get going too..." I said...

"Are you sure Starr? It's still early..." Beautiee said...

"I need to get home – in case Mommy calls again..."

"Don't you have your phone forwarded to your cell?"

"Yes... but... I just need to get home..."

"Okay Starr..." my father said as he grabbed his keys...

"No Daddy – I'm taking the bus…"

"Starr – let me take you home…"

"Daddy – I wanna take the bus…"

"Why?"

"Honey – let her go…" Beautiee said…

"Alright – Starr – are you sure?"

"Yes Daddy!" I laughed…

"Call me when you get home…"

"Okay Daddy…"

"I love you Starr…" my father said as he pulled me into a hug…

"I love you too Daddy…"

"See you soon…" Beautiee said as she hugged me…

"See you soon…" I said. I started to leave and Daddy stopped me again…

"Starr?"

"Yes Daddy?"

"Here…" he said as put a key in my hand… "Use it in case of an emergency…"

"Okay Daddy – bye!" I yelled and then I went to get the bus…

"Why wouldn't she let me take her home?"

"She needs time to think…" Beautiee answered…

"How do you know that? Did something happen?"

"Yes Bazil – something happened – between us girls…"

"Oh… I see… do I need to be worried?"

"No Bazil…"

"Thank God…"

"You're welcome…" God said…

"I told Starr how we met..."

"You did? Why?"

"Because she asked me..."

"Okay..."

"I told her how you saved my life that night..."

"You told her?"

"I told her that's why when you asked me to marry you the next day – I said yes..."

"What did she say?"

"She asked me did I love you..."

"What did you tell her?" Bazil asked as he pulled Beautiee into his arms and kissed her...

"I told her... yea..." Beautiee said and then they went upstairs...

"Next time I'll let Daddy give me a ride home..." I said to myself as I rode the Coastal Link. "Oh well – I guess I'll enjoy the tour..." I said as we went through Milford and then Stratford. "Oh my God – Bridgeport – finally!" I said as I recognized my surroundings. I couldn't wait to get off the bus when I arrived at the station... "Shoot – there goes the #6 – I'll have to hold it until I get home..." I said as I ran to get the #6 to Trumbull Gardens... "Whew! Made it! Thank God!" I sit as I went to sit down...

"You're welcome..." God said...

"My stop – finally!" I said as I got up to get off...

"Have a good night..." the driver said as I ran off the bus, down the block, and up the stairs to my apartment. As soon as I got in the door, my phone started ringing... "Shit!" I said out loud as I grabbed the phone... "Hello?" I gasped as I took the phone into the bathroom with me and sat down to pee...

"You have a collect call from an Inmate at the Bridgeport Correctional Facility – do you accept the charges?"

"Yes I do..." I said as I wiped myself, got up, and flushed the toilet...

"Hey Starr..."

"Hi Mommy – hold on..." I put the phone down, washed and dried my hands, took the phone, and went to sit in the living room...

"Starr? You there?"

"Yes Mommy – I'm here..."

"You okay?"

"Yes Mommy..."

"How was your day?"

"I had a really good day Mommy..."

"Aww... that's nice – tell me..."

"Well – Daddy came to pick me up..."

"Yea... I know..."

"We went to his house and I met Beautiee..."

"You did? Was she nice?"

"Mommy... she's really nice..."

"Told ya..."

"Mommy..."

"Yes Starr?"

"I asked Daddy what happened..."

"You did?"

"Yea..."

"What's wrong?"

"He said Beautiee tried to kill him – did you know that?"

"Yes Starr..."

"She seems so nice..."

"She is Starr..."

"Are you sure Mommy?"

"What did your father say?"

"He told me to let it go..."

"Then that's what you should do..."

"Okay Mommy... if you say so..."

"So you met Beautiee..."

"Yea – we had coffee – and then we went to the Golden Corral!"

"Nice!"

"Then we went to his publishing company! I didn't know Daddy had a publishing company – and Mommy – guess what?"

"What?"

"Beautiee writes books too – and she works with Daddy!"

"Oh wow – that's nice..."

"Mommy – Daddy told them he wanted to introduce his children – me and Baby Osgood..."

"Baby Osgood? Beautiee's pregnant?"

"Yes!"

"Oh wow..."

"Mommy – Beautiee showed me around – and she told everyone I was her daughter..."

"Aww..."

"Daddy hired Sheila, then her daughter, then her son-in-law – maybe I can work there too... I hope..."

"I hope not..."

"Why not Mommy?"

"Nothing – I just want you to find a job where your father is not your boss – it can be tricky..."

"Mommy – we went back to Daddy's house – and I met Keisha and Troy..."

"Who are they?"

"The neighbors – Mommy – Keisha is funny!"

"What makes you say that?"

"As soon as she met me she asked me if I was fuckin' Chandler!" I laughed...

"What? You should've asked her if she was fuckin'!"

"I did Mommy – and she said le'me tell you somthin' lil' girl – I been fuckin' my husband since the first night I saw him!"

"No shit!" my mother laughed...

"She said she just knew..."

"Sometimes you do..."

"I told them that's how I felt about Chandler..."

"I know – don't remind me..."

"I was right about Chandler Mommy..."

"Yes you were..."

"Mommy – Beautiee told me what it was like when she met Daddy..."

"Really?"

"She said she was at the bar and she asked Daddy who are you and he said I'm Your Thirst Quencher..."

"Your father always had a smooth tongue..."

"Beautiee said she went to Daddy's room and told him she needed to take a shower – Daddy undressed her –she had bruises – and Mommy – guess what else?"

"What Honey?"

"Daddy cut his hand in the shower because Beautiee had glass in her hair..."

"Damn! What the hell happened to her?"

"Somebody beat her up Mommy... and Daddy took care of her..."

"Your father fell in love with her..."

"Beautiee said he saved her life that night..."

"Aww..."

"Beautiee said that's why when Daddy asked her to marry him the next day – she said yes..."

"Wait... what?"

"Mommy – she only knew Daddy for 24 hours – I asked her did she love Daddy – she said yes..."

"She was telling you the truth Starr..."

"How do you know Mommy?"

"Because your father makes women fall for him..."

"Mommy?"

"Yes Starr?"

"Did you love Daddy?'

"Yes..."

"Did Daddy love you?"

"Starr – your father loved his wife..."

"Daddy told me he cared about you..."

"He did..."

"I don't think Beautiee tried to kill Daddy..."

"I don't think so either..."

"She loves Daddy too much... I can feel it..."

"There you go being sensitive..."

"That's what Beautiee said..."

"When did she say that?"

"She said that today when I told her I could feel she was pregnant – she said I'm a sensitive..."

"I'm starting to see why your father fell in love with her..."

"Really Mommy?"

"She's a sensitive too..."

"Oh wow..."

"At least I know I won't have to worry when you're with her..."

"I wonder if Daddy's a sensitive?"

"He must be – 'cause you damn sure didn't get it from me!" my mother laughed...

"I wish you were here Mommy..."

"I'll be out soon..."

"You will?"

"Yea – my parole was granted..."

"Mommy! Oh my God!"

"I still have to go to the shelter – but at least I can see you – I can't wait..."

"Me either..."

"Mary – times up..."

"Okay – Starr – I gotta go – I love you..."

"I love you too Mommy!" I said and then I hung up. "I'm gonna talk to my father..." I said out loud. "Oh shoot – I was supposed to call him and let him know I got home – let me do that before I forget..." I said as I dialed the number... "Hmmm... no answer – oh well... I'll call him back later...." I said out loud as I hung up.

Chapter 13

"Oh Bazil... Yess... Fuck me..."

"Like this?" Bazil asked as he grabbed Beautiee by her ass and thrust upward...

"Oh God... Yess... just like that..."

"I sure hope Daddy doesn't get mad at me for coming over so early... oh well... if they're still sleep I'll just go make myself some coffee..." I said out loud as I let myself in...

"Uggh! Uggh! Uggh! Uggh!"

"Bazil... Bazil... Bazil..."

"Oh shit! Daddy! What's wrong!" I cried as I went running upstairs... and ran to the bedroom...

"Beautiee..."

"Bazil..."

"Starr..."

"Oh my God – I'm sorry – I'm so embarrassed!" I yelled as I ran downstairs...

152

"Beautiee... wait!" I heard my father yell but Beautiee was already on her way downstairs...

"Little girl..." she growled when she saw me. She was so mad – her face was red and her nostrils were flaring...

"Yes... Beautiee?"

"In the kitchen – now!"

"Okay Beautiee..." I said as I followed her into the kitchen and sat at the table...

"You want some coffee?" she asked. I could see she calmed down a little but I could tell she was still mad...

"Yes... please..." I watched Beautiee put the pot on, pour in the water, and put the coffee in the Keurig.

"I'm making hazelnut – is that alright or do you want French vanilla?"

"I'll take the hazelnut..."

"Come sit here..." she said as she patted the chair for me to sit next to her at the island...

"Okay..." I sat down in the chair next to her and waited for her to start yelling at me but she didn't...

"Bazil?"

"Yes Beautiee?"

"I'm making coffee..."

"Okay – I'll be right down..."

"Oh God..." I thought to myself... "I really screwed up..."

"It's not that serious..." God said as my father came into the kitchen and sat down at the island next to me...

"Good morning Beautiful..." he said as he kissed me on my forehead...

"Good morning Daddy..." I said as I smiled. We both looked at Beautiee and she wasn't smiling. She put three cups of coffee on the island – one in front of me, one in front of my father, and one for herself. She didn't speak and neither did we. I watched Beautiee go in the fridge, take out the hazelnut flavored creamer, put it on the island in front of us, and then she sat down. She poured some hazelnut creamer in her coffee then pushed it in front of me so I could pour some in mine. My father poured some in his cup and then we all just started drinking our coffee. Beautiee finished her coffee first and then she spoke...

"Good morning Starr..."

"Good morning Beautiee..."

"How did you get in here?"

"My father gave me a key... in case of an emergency..."

"I see..." Beautiee sighed. I looked at my father and he just put his head down... "So... what brings you by here so early... what's wrong?"

"Well..." I answered as I started crying... "My mother is being released today... and I really don't want her to go to the shelter... I want her to come home..."

"I'm sorry Starr... your mother's going to have to go to the shelter..." my father said...

"Daddy... please... isn't there anything you can do?"

154

"Starr... you know I love you with all my heart... but there's nothing I can do..."

"Daddy... please... I know I'll lose my Section 8... can't you help me pay the rent so Mommy can stay with me? Please?"

"Starr... no..."

"It's not fair!" You said you would help me!"

"Yes... I did... but I'm not helping your mother Starr... I'm sorry..."

"Daddy please... just until I get a job..."

"Starr..." my father answered as he took my hand and kissed it... "I love you... but the answer is no..."

"Fine!" I snapped and then I got up to leave...

"Little girl - get your ass back in here and sit the fuck down!" Beautiee yelled. I stopped dead in my tracks and turned around. I waited for my father to say something but he didn't. "You didn't hear what the fuck I said?" Beautiee asked as she started to get up... I figured I better hurry up and sit back down so I did – I sat right back next to my father... "First of all – don't ever disrespect your father like that again..."

"Yes Beautiee... sorry Daddy..."

"Second – if you have an emergency – you call before you come over here..."

"What if you don't answer the phone?"

"Do you have your father's cell phone number?"

"Yes..."

"Do you have my cell phone number?"

"No..."

"Give me your phone..."

"Okay..." I said as I took my phone out my pocket and gave it to her. I watched Beautiee put her phone number in my phone and save it, and then she gave my phone back to me...

"If we don't answer the phone – you call your father on his cell – you leave a message that you have an emergency – you let him know you need him to call you right back – if he doesn't call you right back – you call me on my cell – you leave me the same message – if I don't call you right back then – and only then – do you use your key to let yourself in here – and – when you do let yourself in here – you say Beautiee – Dad – are you here – do you understand me?"

"Yes Beautiee... I understand..."

"Good – now what time is your mother getting released?"

"1 p.m. this afternoon..."

"Okay – go home and get ready to pick up your mother – I'm going to have a discussion with your father..." Beautiee said as she got up, pulled me out the chair, and hugged me...

"Thank you Beautiee..." I said as I hugged her back...

"How are you getting your mother?"

"I'm going to take the bus..."

"Do you have money for you and you're mother to get on the bus?"

"Yes..." I said as I started to leave...

"Excuse me – where do you think you're going?" my father exclaimed...

"I'm... I'm going to get ready... to get my mother...

"I don't get a hug?" I don't get a good bye?"

"Sorry Daddy..." I said as I went over to my father and gave him a hug...

"That's better..."

"Okay Daddy – bye..." I said as I left.

"I love you Mrs. Osgood..." Bazil said as he pulled Beautiee into a kiss...

"Mmmm... I love you too... and we have some unfinished business..." she said as she pushed Bazil back into the chair..."

"This chair's kinda high... are you sure you can do this?" Bazil breathed as Beautiee straddled him and slid down on his dick...

"Only one way to find out... hold on..." she said as she wrapped her arms around his neck, threw her head back, and started riding his dick... "Oh shit... Bazil... Fuck..."

"Beautiee... Damn..." Bazil moaned as he grabbed her ass and pulled her to him...

"Bazil... Fuck me..."

"Beautiee..." Bazil moaned as he pulled her face to his and kissed her...

"Huh... Huh... Huh..." Beautiee moaned in his mouth. Bazil put his tongue in her mouth kissed her harder, and continued fucking her as the chair began to rock... "Oh God Bazil... I'm cumming..."

"Uggh! Uggh! Uggh!" Bazil growled as he grabbed Beautiee behind her back and held her tighter...

"Huh... Huh... Huh..."

"Fuuuccckkk!" Bazil growled as he thrust himself in her harder...

"Bazileee!" Beautiee moaned as she buried her face in his neck. Bazil held Beautiee and kissed her as their orgasms subsided... "I love these fuckin' chairs..." Beautiee breathed as they continued kissing... "I don't wanna get down..."

"Don't get down then..."

"I need to pee... this baby's pushing down on my bladder..." she said as she got up off his lap..."

"Okay then..." Bazil laughed as he stood up...

"Come upstairs with me..."

"Are we going back to bed?" Bazil asked as he pulled her into a kiss...

"Not yet... we need to talk..."

'Okay..." Bazil said as he held her and started backing her out of the kitchen, through the living room, and to the stairs...

"Bazil... I'm going to trip..."

"No you won't... I gotchu..." he said as he pushed her onto the stairs...

"Bazil..." she breathed...

"Spread your legs..." he breathed as he laid himself on top of her...

"Bazil... I can't... I need to go pee..." Bazil didn't pay her any mind... he kissed her and eased himself inside her... "Bazil..."' she moaned...

"Yes... Beautiee..." he moaned as he held her back and continued thrusting... Beautiee gave in and wrapped her legs around Bazil, clasped her feet around his back, held on, and kissed him... "Mmph! Mmph! Mmph!"

"Mmmm! Mmmm! Mmmm!"

"Mmph! Mmph! Mmph!"

"Mmmm! Mmmm! Mmmm!" they moaned into each other's mouths...

"Bazil... I'm cumming again..."

"I'm cumming with you..." he moaned as he thrust harder..."

"Oh shit... Bazileee!" she screamed as she dug her nails into the small of his back and came... and so did the pee... 'Bazil..."

"Yes... Beautiee..."

"I'm soaking wet..."

"Yes... you are..." Bazil breathed as he kissed her neck...

"Bazil... I know what you're doing..."

"Beautiee..." Bazil breathed as he kissed her...

"Bazil... I... need... to... take... a shower..."

"Can I come? Again?"

"Yes... but..." Bazil didn't pay Beautiee any mind... he held her close, picked her up, pulled himself up by the banister... and carried her upstairs with her legs still locked behind him, into the bedroom, and into the shower. Once in the shower Beautiee dropped the robe and Bazil pushed her back into the corner of the shower and turned on the water... "Bazil..."

"Yes... Beautiee..."

"You know I love you..."

"Yes…"

"We need to talk…"

"Right now… we need to fuck…" he said as he started thrusting inside her again… "Isn't that right?"

"Yes… My Thirst Quencher…" she moaned…

"And… you need to cum again… don't you?"

"Oh God… yes…"

"Cum for me…" Bazil growled as he started fucking her harder…

"Oooohhh…. Bazil… Fuck…"

"Uugh! Uugh! UUgh!"

"Bazil… Bazil… Bazil…"

"Uugh! Uugh! Uugh! Now…" he breathed as he kissed her… "You said something… about… talking?"

"Yes… Bazil…"

"Okay… talk to me…" he said and then he kissed her again…

"Mmmm…. Bazil…"

"Yes… Beautiee…"

"Stop…"

"Is… that… what… you… really… want?"

"No…"

"I… didn't… think… so…"

"Bazil…"

"Yes… Beautiee…"

"Please…"

"Okay… under one condition…"

"Yes…"

"When... we're... done...talking... we're... going... back... to... fucking... and... you're... going... to... let... me... fuck... you... for... the... rest... of... the... day... understand?"

"Yes... My Thirst Quencher... yes..."

"Mmmm... good... now... let's... get... outta... here... so... we... can... get... back... in... here..." he said as he kissed her left breast... "Here..." he said as he kissed her right breast... "And especially... here..." he said as he lowered himself down to her pussy and kissed her clit...

"Oh Bazil... yesss..."

"Oh no..." he said as he got up and turned off the water... "You said we need to talk remember?" he laughed.

Chapter 14

"Hey Chan..." I said as I walked up to him...

"Hey!" Chandler exclaimed. I pulled him into a kiss so fast it startled him..."Damn..." he breathed...

"How... much... time... do... we... have?" I asked between kisses...

"I'm... the... Sergeant..." he said between kisses, and then he picked me up and carried me into the bedroom... "We have all the time you need..." he said and then he dropped me on the bed...

"Take off your clothes..."
"Yes Maam..." Chandler laughed as he began to take off his clothes...

"Come here..." Chandler came over to me and I reached out to touch him. Chandler stood there and watched me run my hands up and down his body without saying anything. He smiled when I started stroking his dick with both hands...

"Oh... okay... I see what time it is..." Chandler said as he came towards me...

"Come sit up here..." I said as I patted the bed where I wanted him to sit... "Move back against the headboard..."

"Okay..." Chandler said as he pushed himself back against the headboard. I turned to face him, got on my knees, straddled him, and eased myself down on his dick...

"Ooohhh..." I moaned as Chandler started pushing himself further up inside me...

"Oh shit..." Chandler moaned as he held me close to him and fucked me...

"Chandler... Ooohhh... Chandler..." I moaned. I threw my head back and Chandler kissed and licked on my neck, turning me on and turning me up... "Oh God... Chandler..." Chandler took my left breast in his mouth, increased his intensity, and moaned while he was sucking...

"Mmmph! Mmmph! Mmmph!"

"This feels so good... Chandler..." I moaned. Chandler moved his mouth from my left breast to my right, put it in his mouth... and sucked hard... "Chandler... Chandler... Chandler... Ooohhh..."

"Mmmph! Mmmph! Mmmph!"

"I'm cumming Chandler!"

"Mmmph! Mmmph! Mmmph!"

"Ahh! Ahh! Ahh!"

"Mmmmmpppphhhhh!!!" Chandler moaned as he buried his head in my shoulder. Chandler continued holding me as he pulled my face to his, put his tongue in my mouth, and kissed me hard...

"Now I know why Beautiee was so mad..."
I breathed...

"Wait... what?" Chandler asked. I got down off of Chandler and lay down next to him. Chandler lay down next to me and pulled me close to him so I could lie on his chest. He wrapped his arm around me and I started playing with his dick... "Uh Uh..." he said as he moved my hand...

"Chandler..."

"Starr... talk to me..."

"Okay... please don't be mad..."

"Why would I be mad?"

"Because... I saw something... and I wanted to try it... with you..."

"Aww... that's sweet..." Chandler said as he turned to face me, pulled me close, and kissed me...

"I saw... my father... and Beautiee..."

"Oh shit – you caught them fuckin'?"

"Yea..."

"And Beautiee was doing to your father what you did... to me?"

"Yea..."

"So... you liked what you saw..."

"I was so embarrassed..."

"But you still liked it..."

"I thought my father was having a heart attack... so I ran upstairs... and I saw them..."

"You never heard people having sex before?"

"No..."

"What about your mother?"

"Never..."

"I get it... so why did you say you understand why Beautiee was so mad?"

"Because... she was feeling like you made me feel... and I interrupted... so she didn't..."

"You think she didn't come?"

"Yea..."

"Starr..." Chandler said as he kissed me... "I have so much to teach you..." he laughed...

"What's so funny?"

"Le'me ask you a personal question..."

"Okay..."

"You ever masturbate?"

"Chandler! That's personal!"

"Have you?"

"Yea..."

"You ever get caught?"

"No... if I heard my mother coming I'd stop..."

"Did you ever go back and finish?"

"Sometimes..."

"You don't need to worry about Beautiee..."

"Oohhh... okay... I got it!"

"If we're ever interrupted before we can finish...." he said as he started kissing my neck... "We can always go back and finish later..." he said as he put his hand between my legs and started playing with my clit...

"Oh Chandler..." I moaned as he pushed me on my back, put his tongue in my mouth, kissed me harder, and continued to play with my clit... "Mmmm.... Mmmm... Mmmm..." I moaned as he stuck his fingers in my pussy, pulled them out, and played with my clit harder... "Mmmm! Mmmm! Mmmm!" I screamed in his mouth as I arched my back and came up off the bed. Chandler continued applying pressure to my clit as my legs shook and I dropped back down... "Hhmm...hhmmm... hhmmm..." I moaned in Chandler's mouth as he continued playing with my clit softly until I was completely relaxed... "Oh Chandler..." I whispered with tears in my eyes. Chandler kissed my eyes and my mouth... "Can I?" I breathed as I reached for his dick and started playing with it...

"Yessss..." Chandler breathed as he turned on his back and pulled me under his arm so I could lay on his chest... "Starr... yeesss... just like that..." I snuggled under his arm and listened to his heart beat as his dick got hard in my hand... "Oh yeesss... stroke it... mmmm...." Chandler got even harder as I kept stroking and I liked how his dick felt in my hand... "Starr... Fuck... I'm cuming..." he moaned as he rose up off the bed... "Don't stop Starr..." he moaned as he started shaking...

"Chandler..." I breathed as I tightened my grip...

"Starr... Ooohhh.... Fuuuccckkk!" Chandler moaned and I watched his sperm shoot out the tip and run down my hand. It felt warm and I wasn't sure if I should keep going or stop, so I slowed down and kept playing with his dick until he put his hand on mine... "Damn Starr... I'ma let you do that more often..."

"I've never done that before..."

"I have more to teach you..."

"I love these lessons..."

"I know..."

"It felt so good Chandler..."

"I'm glad you enjoyed it..."

"Does it ever stop feeling good?"

"No..."

"I'm glad I waited for you Chandler..."

"I'm glad you did too..." Chandler said as he kissed me again... "Now... tell me what happened this morning..."

"I went to see my father to tell him my mother's getting out today..."

"Okay..."

"My father gave me a key to use in case of an emergency... so I let myself in..."

"You didn't call first?"

"No..."

"I bet you won't do that again..." Chandler laughed.

"I sure won't – Beautiee was so mad – she made me get in the kitchen and made us coffee..."

"I'd be mad too..." Chandler laughed...

"I asked my father to help me pay my rent so my mother could stay with me but my father said he's not doing anything to help my mother...

"Starr..." Chandler said as he pulled my face to him... "Look at me..." He could see the tears in my eyes and he kissed me... "I know this is hard for you... but you need to understand how your father feels...

"I do... but she's my mother..."

"I know Starr... I'm sorry you have to go through this..."

"So am I..."

"So what happened after you drank your coffee?"

"Beautiee told me to call first – and if I use the key I should call out to see if they're home... then she cursed at me..."

"What?"

"She cursed at me..."

"Why?"

"She said I disrespected my father..."

"Did you?"

"Kinda..."

"Oh okay... so what are you going to do?"

"Beautiee gave me a hug, told me to go get my mother, and she's going to have a discussion with my dad..."

"Aww... that's sweet..."

"She really loves my father – doesn't she?"

"Oh yea... and she loves you too..."

"Really?"

"Trust me – if she's willing to have a discussion" he emphasized with his fingers... "with your father – she loves you..."

"Aww... I'm glad... that'll make my mother happy..."

"And it will make your father happy..."

"You think Beautiee will get my father to change his mind?"

"Maybe... but we'll talk about that later – I need to get ready for work..." he said as he jumped up outta bed...

"I'll come back tonight..." I said as I got up, went over to him, and kissed him...

"Don't worry – if you want to spend time with your mom – it's cool – now I gotta get ready..." he said as he went into the bathroom and I followed him into the shower... "Starr... we can't do this now... I'm running late..."

"We can both take a shower – I won't touch you – unless you want me to..." I laughed.

Chapter 15

"Okay Beautiee..." Bazil sighed... "Let's talk..." he said as they sat down at the desk in the library...

"Okay... I'm just going to come out and say this..."

"Go ahead..."

"I love Starr..."

"Oh Beautiee..."

"You love Starr..."

"Of course..."

"You want what's best for her – right?"

"Yesss... I guess..."

"Bazil... please..."

"Okay..."

"Starr's a good girl..."

"Yes... she is..."

"She's managed to stay focused in spite of what she's been through..."

"Yes... she has..."

"We don't want her to lose that..."

"No... we don't..."

"Bazil..."

"Yes Beautiee..."

"Starr needs her mother..."

"I know... but I just can't do it... you don't understand..."

"My Thirst Quencher..." Beautiee said as she pulled his face close to hers and kissed him... "I understand completely... she hurt you... and even though you have me... it still hurts..."

"Yes... it does..." Bazil whispered as he started crying...

"That's one of the reason's you didn't tell me about her... isn't it?"

"Yes..."

"I know..." she whispered as she pulled him into a hug and let him cry on her shoulder... "But we have a beautiful daughter in spite of it..."

"We?"

"Yes... we..."

"How can I help her without helping her mother?"

"You help Starr... Starr's going to help her mother no matter what you say... so don't say anything..."

"She shouldn't have that burden..."

"You're right... but Starr needs to see that for herself..."

"What should I do?"

"Well... for starters... we need to get Starr out of public housing..."

"You're right..."

"Now... I found something I think she'll like..."

"She'll be living with Chandler... Mary's the one that'll be living there..."

"I know..."

"So why should I do this?"

"Because... your daughter should have something in her name besides a Section 8 Certificate..."

"You're right..."

"Take a look at this..." Beautiee said as she turned on the computer, went to realtor.com, and pulled up a property...

"Hmmm... this is cute..."

"I thought so too..."

"It's Downtown Bridgeport..."

"Yes... right near Chandler..."

"So she can see her mother whenever she wants..."

"Exactly..."

"Which will make her happy..."

"Exactly..."

"Which will also make her mother happy..."

"Exactly..."

"It's $65,000 – I'm not spending $65,000 for Mary to have a place to stay Beautiee..."

"Bazil..."

"I won't do it Beautiee..."

"Bazil..."

"Yes Beautiee..."

"You're not spending $65,000 for Mary... you're spending $65,000 so your daughter can invest in real estate..."

"Okay..."

"The common charges, taxes, and insurance are less than $500 a month... Starr can pay that with her unemployment..."

"Hmmm... okay... how do I know she won't turn it over to her mother?"

"You put your name on the title along with hers – this way it can't be transferred without your signature..."

"Damn... I love you..."

"I love you too..."

"What if Starr can't come up with the money?"

"You and Starr can sublet to Mary... Mary's going to be released from prison – she'll go down to DSS – they will pay about $200 or so for rent for her – Starr only needs to come up with the rest..." Bazil put his hand under his chin and sat there thinking... and then he bust out laughing... "What's so funny?"

"Bitch owes me $50,000 – pay me!" he laughed.

"So... you'll do it?"

"Yes... I'll do it..."

"Oh thank God!" Beautiee breathed...

"You're welcome..." God said...

"I'm going to call the realtor right now..."

"Beautiee... wait..."

"You're not changing your mind – are you?" Bazil didn't answer her... he just pulled her close to him, wrapped his arms around her, and kissed her...

"I love you Mrs. Osgood..."

"I love you too..."

"Do... you... remember... my... condition?"

"Yeesss... I remember..."

"So... are... we... done... talking?" he asked as he pulled Beautiee down on top of him and down to the floor...

"No..."

"What... else... do... we... need... to... talk... about?"

"Bazil... I... need... to... make... this... call..."

"I'll... give... you... five... minutes... after that..." he whispered in her ear... "I'm fucking you..."

"Okay... I'll hurry..." she said as she jumped up off the floor and grabbed the phone. Bazil looked at Beautiee and started tapping his watch...

"Hello – Keller Williams Realty – Sharon Lemdon speaking..."

"Ms. Lemdon – high – this is Mrs. Osgood..."

"Hello Mrs. Osgood – how may I help you?"

"My husband would like to put in a cash offer on 46 Oakview Circle – Unit 103 – in Bridgeport – full asking..."

"That's wonderful!" I'll get the offer to you right away!"

"Okay – send it to WJL@OsgoodPublishing.com..."

"I sure will – are you working with a realtor?"

"No..."

"Okay – do you have an attorney?"

"Yes..." Beautiee breathed as Bazil started rubbing her leg...

"Would you like to see the property?"

"Yes..." Beautiee breathed as Bazil stood up and started kissing her on her neck... "Yes..."

"Okay – I can show it to you today at 4pm..."

"Okay – we'll meet you there..." Beautiee breathed... "At 4..." she said as Bazil took the phone from her, hung it up, pulled her into a kiss, and lowered her to the floor...

"Spread your legs..." Bazil breathed as he got on top of her, kissed her neck, and opened her robe... "Oh Bazil... yeesss..." Beautiee moaned as Bazil eased himself inside her and began thrusting while simultaneously sucking her left nipple and then her right...

"Mmmm...." Bazil moaned into Beautiee's mouth as he kissed her...

"Hmmm.....   Hmmm....   Hmmm.... Hmmm...."

Mmmphh!   Mmmphhh!   Mmmphhh! Mmmphh!"

"Hmmm.....   Hmmm....   Hmmm.... Hmmm...."

"Damn you feel good..." Bazil breathed in her ear as he wrapped his arms underneath her, held her tight, and continued fucking her...

"Bazil... Bazil... Bazil... Huh..."

"Does it feel good?"

"Fuck... yesss... yesss...."

"Ugghh! Ugghh! Ugghh!"

"Oh Bazil... I'm cumming... I'm cumming..." Bazil covered Beautiee's mouth with his and thrust his tongue inside...

Mmmphh! Mmmphhh! Mmmphhh! Mmmphh!" Bazil continued to lay there on top of Beautiee... kissing her...

"Oh my God..." Beautiee breathed... "That was so fuckin' intense..."

"Yes... yes it was..."

"I want more..."

"You need to eat..."

"I want more..."

"Let me feed you... and the baby... and then I'll give you more..."

"Mmmm... okay..." Beautiee sighed as Bazil helped her up off the floor and they went into the kitchen.

Chapter 16

"Mommy!" I yelled when I saw her...

"Oh Starr... my baby..." she cried as we hugged each other...

"I missed you so much Mommy..." I cried...

"I missed you more..." she cried...

"Mommy – let's go – I have so much to tell you..."

"Damn I'm hungry..."

"I have some money Mommy – we can go eat..."

"You gonna take me out? To eat?"

"Yes Mommy – hurry up – the bus is coming!"

"Okay! Where we goin'?"

"Wait!" I yelled as the bus pulled up to the stop...

"I'm comin' Starr – hang on – I'm not as young as I used to be..." she laughed as she tried to run across the street but ended up walking...

"Thank you for waiting..." I said as I got on the bus...

"You're welcome – you need a transfer?"

"I need two all day passes..." I said as my mother got on the bus... "Go sit down Mommy – I got it..."

"Okay... whew..." she said as she sat down and I put the money in...

"Here ya go lil' lady..." the bus driver said as he handed me the passes...

"Thank you..." I said as I took the passes and went to sit with Mommy..."

"Oh my God – you look so good... you're glowing... things must be great between you and Chandler. I didn't say anything... I just held up my hand... "Oh my God! He proposed?"

"Yes Mommy!"

"Oh my God – my baby's getting married!"

"Yes Mommy!" I yelled as we held each other and cried...

"I can't be out too long – I need to check in at the shelter..."

"No you don't Mommy..."

"Starr... what are you not telling me?"

"Mommy – let's go eat – I'll tell you everything then..."

"Okay – my God – you're so beautiful – I love you so much..."

"I love you too Mommy..."

"Where we goin?"

"Where you wanna go?"

"Let's go to Red Lobster – is that alright?"

"Yes Mommy – that's fine..."

"Oh my God – I can taste it now – thank you..."

"You're welcome Mommy..." We didn't talk anymore. I watched Mommy smiling as she looked out the window and it made me so happy... "Almost there..." I said...

"I see it!" Mommy exclaimed...

"Have a nice day Ladies..." the bust driver said as he pulled up to the stop...

"Thank you – we will..." Mommy said...

"What's the special occasion? Is it your birthday?" he asked...

"Yea – it's her birthday!" I yelled before he could ask any more questions. When we got off the bus Mommy started crying... "Mommy – what's wrong?"

"Nothing baby – I'm happy..." she said as she pulled me into a hug.

"I'm happy to Mommy..."

"I know..." she cried...

"C'mon – let's cross the street and get a table – I can't wait to tell you everything!" I said as I took her hand and pulled her across the street to the restaurant...

"Welcome to Red Lobster – how may I help you?"

"Table for two please..." I answered...

"Right this way – is this your mom?"

"Yes – this is my Mommy..."

"Oh how sweet – she still calls you Mommy..."

"Yes – she's very sweet – she's taking me out for my birthday..."

"Oh that's nice..." she said as she set our table and winked at me... "The waitress will be right over..."

"Oh shoot – hang on Mommy... Hi Beautiee... uh huh... okay... bye..."

"What did she want?"

"She was just calling to see if I was okay..."

"Oh... that was nice..."

"I told her I was picking you up and she asked me if I had enough money..."

"Really?"

"Yup..."

"So I guess you've been in touch with your dad..."

"Yes Mommy..."

"How is he?"

"He's fine..."

"Was he happy to see you?"

"Are you ready to order?" the waitress interrupted...

"Mommy – do you know what you want?"

"I want a strawberry daiquiri – and I want to taste the liquor..." Mommy laughed...

"Okay – and you?" she asked me...

"I'll just have ginger ale..."

"Have a drink with your Mommy – we're celebrating..."

"Okay – I'll have a strawberry daiquiri too..."

"Coming right up... I'll be back with your drinks..." she said as she walked away...

"Rude Bitch..." Mommy mumbled...

"Mommy!"

"She was rude – didn't say hi or nuthin' – but anyway – about your dad..."

"Mommy – let's look at the menu first..."

"Okay – I want the ultimate feast with Caesar salad and the sweet potato – this way I get it all – lobster tail, shrimp, and crab legs..."

"Okay Mommy – I'll have that too..."

"Are you ready to place your order?" the waitress asked...

"Yea – two ultimate feasts – with Caesar salad and sweet potato..."

"The sweet potato is $2.99 extra – is that okay?"

"Starr?"

"Yes Mommy – that's fine..."

"Okay – here's your daiquiris – I'll place your orders..." the waitress said and then walked away...

"Tell me about your dad..."

"Mommy... Chandler came to see me... after he told me to leave..."

"Okay..."

"He loves me Mommy..."

"You're engage Starr... I get that..."

"He told me he had a surprise for me – he took me to his place – and Daddy was there..." I said as I started crying...

"Aww..." Mommy said as she touched my hand..."

"We hugged each other, we cried, and he told me he always loved me..."

"That's nice..."

"He said he would help me Mommy..."

"That's good..."

"Mommy..." I whispered as I started crying...

"Starr... what's wrong?"

"Chandler told Daddy he was in love with me..."

"Aww..."

"And then he... he..."

"What happened baby?"

"He told Daddy he wanted to marry me..." I cried...

"Oh Starr!"

"And... then... he... asked Daddy... for his blessing..." I cried as I picked up the napkin and wiped my nose...

"And your father said yes..." Mommy sighed...

"Chandler told me to stand up... and then he got down on one knee... and he proposed..."

"Hot damn – my baby is engaged to the Sergeant of the Bridgeport Police!"

"I met Daddy's wife – I love her..."

"Really?"

"She's really nice – and she really loves Daddy..." I laughed...

"What makes you say that?"

"Here's some biscuits..." the waitress interrupted...

"Mommy... I caught them..." I said as we each took a biscuit and started eating...

"You caught them?"

"Yes Mommy – they were having sex..." I laughed...

"No shit!"

"I was so embarrassed..."

"Girl – you fuckin' aintcha?"

"Yes Mommy – but..."

"That's how you got here honey!" Mommy laughed...

"Mommy... I heard Daddy... I thought something was wrong... I ran upstairs... and... I saw them..."

"Starr – you've never seen sex on tv?"

"Yes Mommy – but..."

"Girl – what happened?"

"I tried to run... but Beautiee came downstairs after me... and made me go in the kitchen..."

"Oh shit – she let you have it huh?"

"Kinda..."

"You should'a called first – was your father mad?"

"Not really..."

"What did Beautiee say?"

"She made us coffee – then she asked me how I got in the house – I told her Daddy gave me a key in case of an emergency..."

"Honey – what was so urgent that you had to go over there so damn early?"

"You Mommy..."

"Me?"

"Yes Mommy – I went over there to ask Daddy to help me pay my rent so you could stay with me... and he said no... so I got mad... and Beautiee cursed at me..."

"Wait – what?"

"I got mad..."

"Skip to the part where Beautiee cursed at you!"

"She told me get my ass back here and sit the fuck down..."

"Oh hell no – what did your father say?"

"Nothing..."

"See – I'ma check that Bitch when I see her..."

"Mommy – No!"

"Here's your food..." the waitress interrupted... "If you need anything else, I'll be right over there..."

"And I'm gonna check your father too – nobody speaks to you like that – and his stupid ass..."

"Mommy! Stop it!"

"Okay... but I'ma have a conversation with Beautiee..."

"Mommy – shut up!"

"Have you lost your mind?"

"Beautiee cursed at me because I disrespected Daddy..."

"So what – fuck him – I don't give a damn what you did..."

"Mommy!"

"Sigh... alright alright..."

"Beautiee told me she'll have a conversation..." I emphasized with my fingers... "with Daddy – then she gave me a hug, told me to come get you, and don't worry..."

"I must be drunk!" Mommy laughed...

"Why?"

"Beautiee is going to have a conversation with your father – to help me? Really?"

"No Mommy – she wants to help me – she knows I don't want you to go to the shelter..."

"Hmmm... I'm surprised..."

"That's why I don't want you to say anything..."

"Okay Starr... I won't say anything about her cursing at you – but when I see her I'm gonna thank her for trying to help you..."

"Here we go! One! Two! Three! Happy Birthday to you, Happy Birthday to you, Happy Birthday Dear Mommy.... Happy Birthday to you!"

"Awww... thank you!" Mommy said as the servers left a brownie with vanilla ice cream and a lit candle on the table...

"C'mon Mommy – let's go – I can't wait to go home!" I said as I signaled the waitress to bring the check...

"Starr... my ice cream will melt..."

"Mommy – there's a bakery downtown where we get off the bus – I'll buy you a cake – and I have ice-cream in the house – c'mon!"

"Okay, okay!" Mommy laughed.

<u>Twisted Starr Tree</u>

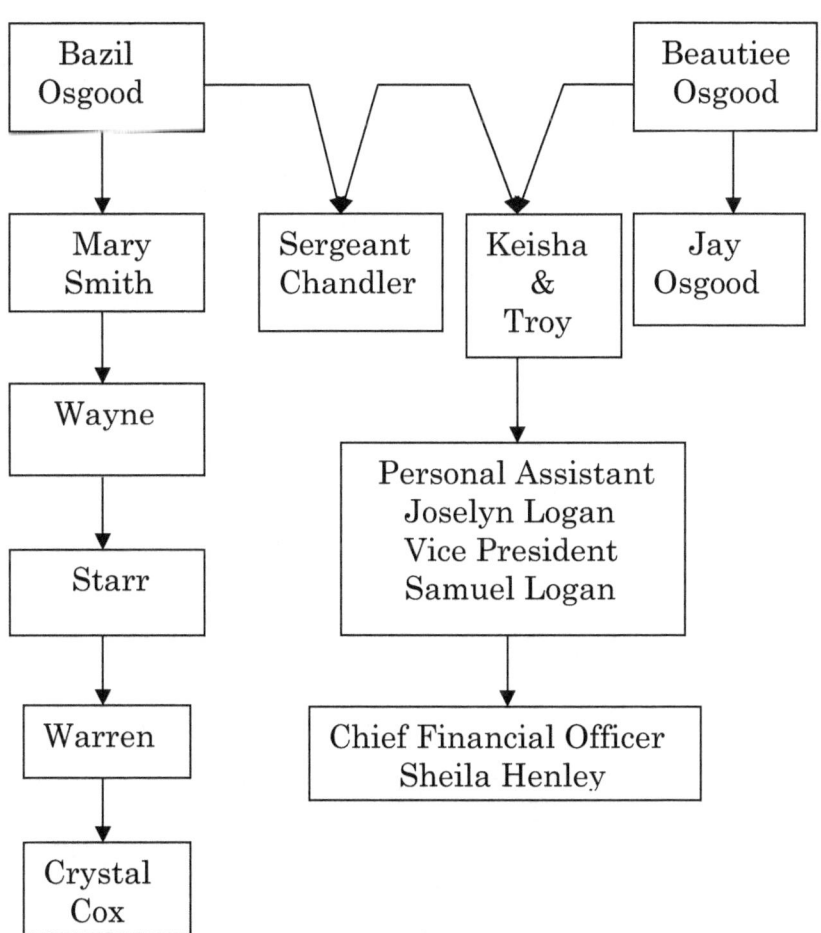